GIVEN T
GARG

Ami Wright

ONE

William

My mind is sluggish these days. That doesn't stop me from noticing when *she* walks across centerstage at the Grand Theater. The brunette's lithe beauty catches my eye from my rooftop perch where I have a view through the glass dome above her. My vision is sharper than it was when I was human. I can see in the dark better than I used to as well. So I have no trouble narrowing in on her shapely legs where they peek from the long dark jacket she wears. She strides to the front of the stage and stops.

The woman looks around. I can't tell what she's looking for. The theater is empty. It's evening, but there's no show on tonight. There hasn't been a show since the threats escalated. Not that I care. I prefer it that way.

I wonder what she's doing here. She fishes a small metallic device I recognize as a phone from her purse, sets a song playing, and puts down her things on the edge of the stage. A rhythmic, sensuous beat plays and she sways her hips. It seems like decades since I even moved my head, but you'd better believe I move it then. I swivel my head all the way to the right for a better look at her fingers slipping up the seam of her jacket, unfastening each button one by one.

If I wasn't already literally fixed in place, I would be now.

She slides the jacket over her shoulders and casts it aside, revealing pert breasts cupped in a lacy black bra. Tight black shorts ride low over curvy hips. She's still wearing her stiletto heels and they make her legs look amazing when she turns and bends at the waist, giving me an exquisite view of her juicy rounded backside where the tiny shorts absolutely do nothing to cover it. I stare as she runs her hands down the front of her legs slowly, and then she flicks her long, auburn hair back over one shoulder and straightens.

My god, she's gorgeous. I've seen many women—fucked many women—in my lifetime. Most of them before I was cursed, of course.

None of them—not a single one—has ever captured my attention the way this woman does with just a flick of her hair and the sway of her hips. A few simple movements and the shape of her body is etched into my memory. I can feel my heart pounding inside a chest I thought had turned to stone years ago.

Her hands caress up her sides, sliding past breasts I long to feel for myself. She brings them back down her body and toys with the waistband of the tiny shorts. She pulls the shorts down a few inches until I'm sure I catch a glimpse of a smooth, bare mound. Then the shorts are back in place and she's turning, swaying, dancing to the music. She continues her deliberate torment. Does she know she has an audience?

Bending and sliding onto the floor, she kicks out her legs, spreading them wide. All sorts of wicked thoughts flick through my mind. She rolls to her front, rocking and thrusting her hips until I can't do anything but picture her over me, chasing pleasure as she uses my body in just such a way.

I'm riveted to the spot, or I'd be through that glass dome to snatch her up in my arms and carry her away with me. She's lucky. There's no way I'd be able to hold back from doing all the filthy, carnal things her dance has put into my head if I actually had her in my arms.

My breath catches in my throat when she turns her back, unfastening the bra and pulling first one arm then the other free while keeping her hands over her breasts. My mouth waters as she spins with a coy smile. Then she drops her hands and lets me see the most perfect dusky pink nipples.

My hand flexes at my side and I look down, surprised. The movement is fleeting, but it's more than I've been able to do in many, many months. My hand isn't the only thing to move. Between my thighs, my cock juts up proudly, hard and ready. Wretched thing is taunting me. I'm all but frozen into stone, yet there's always a way for it to be worse.

With a sigh, I look back to the stage, where my pretty brunette is bending forward, tugging down her shorts to reveal a luscious ass, perfectly proportioned to give a man a two good handfuls as he thrusts into her from behind.

God's troth, I haven't been this wound up in years.

Too soon it's over. She stops the music and collects her clothing from where it's strewn around the stage. She puts each item back on and ties the belt of the jacket around her waist. Then she strides out of my sight and I'm left longing for more.

Dark laughter to my right makes me glance around. Sethos leans against the tower where I perch, his dark wings folded behind his back and long, leonine tail flicking against his furry leg. A brow lifts on his handsome face as he smirks at me. "So there is something still capable of getting your attention, I see."

I roll my eyes. "Spare me. A man would have to be dead not to notice her."

"Ah, but you're not a man, are you, my friend? Not anymore."

A growl rumbles in my chest and my claws dig into the stone archway where my left hand rests. "I'm not your friend, either."

Sethos chuckles again. "Better and better. A few more nights and we'll have you up and moving again."

"I assume this means I have you to thank for that little show?"

"Naturally. Can't have my investment going to waste, can I? I told you when I had you shipped here that I needed someone to guard my theater. I'm not running a charity here."

I turn my gaze away from the sphinx and down to the street, hoping to catch a glance at the woman as she leaves the theater. Not like he ever asked me what I thought about my current living and working arrangements. Who asks the stonework what it thinks? There I was, perfectly satisfied to wallow in my own misery, ready to be demolished along with my cathedral, when he up and bought me at auction like a fucking Michelangelo or something.

Ha! Far from it. Even in stone, my ugly hide is pockmarked with battle scars and imperfections. The tip of one horn is broken, and I'm fairly sure my wings are cracked. I'll probably never fly again.

Who am I kidding? I'll never do anything again. I'm too far gone. Sethos is a fool for thinking he can rouse me. Rousing a gargoyle in the process of petrifaction is next to impossible. Apart from anything else, he has to want to be roused, and I've got nothing to live for.

Still, as the saying goes, a fool and his money are soon parted. Who am I to tell this idiot how to throw away his cash? Seems like he has plenty to throw.

Eventually he gives up trying to engage me in any further conversation and leaves. I spend the next few hours staring up and down the street, knowing I won't see her, but hoping anyway. When I drift into my morning sleep, it's to dreams of the pretty brunette. She creeps up the steps to my tower, crawls into my lap, and rocks her sinful hips over me. All the while, she clings to my neck and whispers sweet nothings in my ear.

TWO

Jessie

Weirdest request I've had in a long time. Strip in an empty theater at night time. Not even any music. Luckily I'm always prepared.

As I dress and collect my things, I can't shake the feeling of eyes on me, but when I take another long look around the theater, I still can't see anyone.

Shrugging it off, I pull the door closed behind me as the instructions said to do and head down Hart Row. It's still quite warm. Not really cold enough for even the light jacket I'm wearing, but I wanted to keep things simple for my performance. Since I've got nothing but underwear on underneath it, I'll be leaving the jacket on, thank you very much. I'm not giving it away for free!

I step onto the subway and flick open the Monstrous Deals app on my phone. Well, that's one thing that's gone right today. My mysterious client has already sent through the payment for tonight. I guess someone was in the theater after all. Someone I couldn't see, but they must have seen me. I wonder what monsters can become invisible. I mean, I've had some unusual clients, but never someone invisible before. It's got to be that. Not that I mind. If they're going to pay up and not bother me, I'll take their bookings every time.

I gotta say, monster clients beat human clients any day. At least so far.

I get off at my stop, dragging my feet across the two blocks to the scummy youth hostel where I'm staying. A bed in a six-person dorm is my idea of hell, but it's all I can afford while I'm saving for a security deposit so I can rent my own place.

Throwing my jacket into the locker beneath my bed, I pull on my sweats and tuck my feet up on the lower bunk. I pull the curtain closed and try to block out the snores of the girl in bed above me. Rachel, I think her name is. She probably told me and I promptly forgot it.

She hasn't reached full rattling train car levels yet, but it's only a matter of time.

With a sigh, I flop back on my pillow. Tonight's job was a good start, but it's not enough for the deposit I'll need to move out of this shithole and get a private room. I used up all my savings in my first couple weeks here. I thought I'd get work more easily. I've done dozens of auditions, but nothing has come of them. I'm going to need to make a choice soon. Find a regular nine to five, or go home. Neither option really works for me. I work a regular job and I'll cut down my chances of being available at short notice if something comes up. Going home's not really an option for me right now. Even if I could afford the flight—which I doubt—my parents were pretty clear. If I made the stupid decision to fly halfway across the world to pursue my stupid dream, they were going to wash their hands of me. I'm not sure they'd welcome me back to my old room. Not sure I could stand going back there, anyway. It's shameful enough still living at home at twenty-two, sneaking around trying to pretend I'm not working as a stripper. It'd be worse crawling back with my tail between my legs at twenty-three, having to admit they were right after all.

Well, they're not right. I won't let them be. I'm going to get stage work. Real acting work. I'm going to save up that money. I'm going to get a gig on an ad, or as an extra or something, and things will take off from there. That's where it starts. A job and a room in a shared flat. A private room all to myself! A door I can close and no stinky socks hanging over the edge of the bed in the morning.

Heaven.

It's the small things in life that matter. Small things like being able to come. God, it's been a while. It doesn't matter what time of day or night here, there's always someone awake and I don't have time for hookups right now. Between auditions and odd jobs through Monstrous Deals and another site I use, at the end of the day I don't have it in me to go looking for a guy. If I could use this Monstrous Deals app myself, I would. It would be easier to pay to have someone do whatever you want, rather than have to go looking.

Too bad I'm too poor. And not a monster.

I'm just a human girl looking for a break.

I've thought about offering more than just a dance, but in the end I always decide not to. I like sex. I don't want to spoil that by making it my work.

I sigh. I don't usually get turned on at work. It's just work. But something about tonight was different. Being centerstage in the theater I've dreamed about was thrilling. Being alone without an audience meant I wasn't thinking about what someone else wanted. I was dancing for me. So I focused my mind on what I love about it. What feels good.

I imagined strong hands moving lovingly over my body as I moved. I pictured eyes on me that wanted more than just to devour my image.

A little throb between my legs reminds me how long it's been. Slipping my hand under the waistband of my sweats and into my panties, I groan at how wet I am. Just as I begin making small circles around my aching clit, a snore and the tortured squeak of springs above me makes me suppress a growl of frustration.

Then voices in the hallway get louder until the door bursts open and two drunk girls loudly shush each other over and over while fumbling around the room looking for their bunks.

Pulling my hand from my panties, I roll over and bury my face in my pillow.

I have got to get out of this dorm.

THREE

GIVEN TO THE GARGOYLE

William

I don't know how long I sleep. Sometimes now it's days at a time. I don't even wake for the nights.

When I open my eyes, the city lights glow in the semi-darkness around me, outshining the stars in the heavens. Movement at centerstage catches my eye through the glass dome and I look around.

It's not her.

A woman stands on stage. A pretty young blonde. She's got on a red thong and a matching corset that thrusts her breasts up and nips in her tiny waist. She's moving around the space, swaying her hips and plucking at the tie that fastens the corset at the front.

But it's not *her*.

My gaze isn't drawn to this woman. My claws don't extend to dig into the stone of my perch, and my mouth doesn't water to taste her sweetness.

With a sigh, I close my eyes again.

"Ungrateful bastard." Sethos' tone is mocking.

When I open my eyes again and look, he's leaning in his favorite spot against one of the archways of the tower, idly checking a pointed claw. I know better than to assume a sphinx isn't watching me like a hawk, though.

If I could shrug. I would, but my body is still frozen. I think I have less movement today, in fact. It was probably only my imagination playing tricks on me the other night.

I grunt.

"That's it? That's all the thanks I get for arranging you privately curated entertainment night after night?"

"I never asked you to."

Sethos slinks over and drapes an arm across my shoulders. It makes me smile knowing he has to stretch up on his toes to do it, even though I'm hunched over. He pats my back. "You didn't have to ask. Look at you. Tragic. How can I let you do this to yourself?"

"I wish you'd just butt out," I grumble.

"Not gonna happen. Like I said. Theater needs a guard. You'd be perfect. Just got to find a way to light a fire under you."

I say nothing. Sethos lifts his arm from me and walks across to look down through the glass of the dome. The young blonde is topless now, playing with her breasts as she writhes on the floor. "Is it the fact she's blonde? You like brunettes better, is that it?"

I grunt.

"Well then, what was it about that girl last night that got your attention?"

"What girl?" Maybe if I play dumb, he'll leave me alone. I won't admit just the mention of the girl from last night has my heart beating faster in my chest.

Sethos pulls out his phone and the screen lights up. A moment later he holds it out so I can see the screen. "This one. Jessie. Got you all riled up. Don't pretend she didn't."

I stare at the image of her on the screen. She's wearing a green and black lacy one piece with her hair gathered in a pretty arrangement on top of her head with a few strands trailing loose. Her lips are painted bright red and she smiles as if she's got a secret she'd like to share.

God, how could I have forgotten already how beautiful she is?

Sethos pulls away the phone and I want to reach out to grab his wrist and stop him from doing it. "No. Wait!"

He chuckles. "Oh, so it was her."

"Where did you find her?"

Sethos grins. "I bet you'd like to know that, wouldn't you? But it wouldn't do you any good anyway. Not if you're stuck on that perch like a statue. I could book her for you again. If you like."

I sit there grinding my teeth together, unwilling to let him know just how much I would like to see her again. Jessie. I roll the name around in my mind, determined to remember. I wonder if it's short for something. Jessica. Jesmine. Jesirae.

"You know what I want from you."

Damn prick knows he has me over a barrel. He can probably smell it. Sphinxes are dangerous that way.

I sigh. "You want me to protect the theater."

"I want your word."

"It will be a waste of your effort if all I can do is watch it burn. I'm not much good to you as stone."

Sethos sniffs. "You let me worry about whether I'm wasting my time. Now do I have your word?"

I consider. Gargoyles cannot lie. We cannot break our word once it's given. Sethos knows exactly what he's asking for, because if there's one thing a sphinx knows, it's the power of words.

"Fine," I growl. "I will protect your theater while I'm still perched here." Not like it makes any difference to me. I guarded a damn church for centuries. What's one building over another? Not like God exists. At least I don't think he does. I've never seen any evidence of it in all the time I've been alive.

Magic, yes, but God? No. I still guarded that damn cathedral. Habit, I guess. Fool doesn't realize I'd probably guard the theater even if I didn't give him my word. I mean who wants their bed burning under them?

Sethos smiles. "Then we have an agreement. I'll get you your girl for as long as it takes to wake you up again."

He slinks away, jumping down to the edge of the rooftop and leaping off. Spreading his wings, he glides to the pavement and laughs at the gasps of human pedestrians as he lands. I roll my eyes. Perhaps if he didn't go around showing off so much, people wouldn't want to burn down his theater and attack his patrons. I'll never tell him that, though. It'd be a waste of my breath.

Below me, the blonde has finished and packed up her things. The stage is empty again. I close my eyes and think of Jessie. I wonder what she'll think of being asked to dance for a statue. Would that be better or worse than her knowing the truth? I might be an ugly bastard, but once upon a time that didn't matter. I got enough pussy to keep me happy. And the ladies didn't seem to mind. I made sure to keep them well satisfied so they wouldn't have cause to complain. Now though, when all I can do is watch, I wonder what she'll think of me.

I find myself hoping she doesn't look at my cracked and haggard features with distaste. I haven't cared for years what a single creature thought of me. But I care what Jessie thinks and I can't explain why.

FOUR

Jessie

New message from Monstrous Deals:

Hi Jessie,

We've noticed that you've recently updated your services offered in your profile. That's great! We're always looking for more we can offer our clients. We'd love to chat with you a little more about how things are going for you on Monstrous Deals. It's important that both clients and providers are satisfied at all times. Why don't you book an appointment or simply drop in and see us? The Monster Bar is always open and there's always someone available for a chat day or night.

The Team at Monstrous Deals

Huh. That's kinda nice actually. I've been feeling so shitty about still not getting any acting work I decided to re-evaluate. Sleeping with someone for money doesn't feel so bad. It would certainly be better than working at Macy's and giving up on my dream. And it's waaaay better than crawling home to my parents.

Maybe if I go in and meet with someone from the company, I can get advice about how to make my profile more attractive and pick up more work. I've chatted online with a few girls who say they picked up long-term clients really quickly after signing up. That's the sort of thing I need. An ongoing arrangement so I know where the money's coming from for a while.

Plus they all say their clients treat them well. I wouldn't mind getting in on a bit of that action, too.

Using my elbow and the back of my arm, I brush aside Rachel's damp towel hanging over my bunk and find my shoes. My black heels are looking a little beat up these days, but I can't exactly wear runners to a bar. I pull on the only clean dress I can find, a black bodycon sleeveless dress and hastily pull my long hair into a messy knot on top of my head. A little red lipstick and it'll have to do. I'm low on options because tonight is wash night. I'll deal with that when I get home. Or tomorrow.

It takes me a little while to find the right place. When I step off the subway, I'm pleased to see it's in a nice neighborhood. Quaint little buildings with historical features line the street and the trees in the area are dotted with fairy lights. It looks almost suburban, except the ground floor of most of these buildings is a shopfront.

When I get to the place my phone tells me is the Monster Bar, I think at first something's gone wrong with the GPS. It's a courtyard garden with wrought iron lamps and decorative benches. At the other side of the courtyard is a building painted orange. It has green shutters and a bright yellow door. Surely not.

When I get close enough to ring the buzzer though, I see a little sign which reads 'Monstrous Deals'. There's even a cute little logo with three writhing tentacles just in case you can't work out from the name this place serves supes. I shrug and raise a finger to ring. Before I can, the door opens to reveal a smiling woman with bronze skin and short, pale blonde hair. Her smile grows even wider when she takes me in. "Hi there. Jessie, right?" She holds out her hand and I take it with a frown.

"Um, yeah. How did you—"

She gives me a little laugh. "Well I'm clairvoyant and sometimes these things just come to me, but mostly because I just looked at your file to send out that email. I assume that's why you've come."

"Uh, yeah," I say again. She's so friendly it's hard not to like her instantly, which is unusual for me.

The woman ushers me inside with a wave. "I'm Sofia. Come on in. Can I get you something to drink?"

This is really not what I was expecting. A wooden staircase is off to my left and a door leads toward a cozy sitting room in front of us. Sofia leads me to a sitting room and I settle on a striped sofa and look up at the wall in front of me covered with portraits of beautiful people.

"I really just came to talk to you about getting more clients," I say.

Sofia goes to a little trolley in the corner. "Tea? Coffee? Something stronger?"

I shake my head. "That's OK."

She perches on a white armchair opposite me and folds her hands in her lap with a tinkle from the various golden bangles she's wearing. "So you're looking for more work?"

I nod.

"Anything in particular? Some of our workers are happy with odd jobs, but most people prefer to take on a long-term client. That's usually how our service works best. And I have to say that many of our clients are very generous. They take care of our workers."

I sigh, wishing I hadn't turned down that drink. "But how do I find a client like that?"

Sofia smiles. "They'll find you. Trust me. That's exactly what we do here. But we might be able to speed the process by going downstairs and helping you get to know some of our regulars. Word has a way of spreading. And I have a good feeling for you tonight."

I'd love to say the same, but weeks of failed auditions and no call backs and stinky socks in my face in the morning have worn me down.

Even so, I follow Sofia down the stairs and through a door into a dimly lit space with dark wooden floorboards and booth seating. Little fake candles flicker at scattered tables in the center space. A tall guy with his long blonde hair tied back in a knot stands behind the bar cleaning glasses with a cloth. Sofia leads me over. "Hey, Maurice. This is Jessie. She's a worker. Her first drink is covered, OK?"

Maurice grins and leans on the bar. I can't help noticing how hairy his forearms are. "What'll it be, Jessie?"

"Daquiri, please."

Maurice smiles and I notice the writing on his shirt: 'Call me a good boy'.

"Good choice," he tells me. Then he turns to make the drink and I get to read the back of his shirt. Above an image of a bushy tail, it reads, '...it makes my tail wag'.

Sofia leans in. "Werewolf." She gives me a little nudge and a wink, and I laugh. Of course Maurice is a werewolf. This is the Monster Bar after all.

I look around the bar with fresh eyes, wondering how many other people in here are really supes. I haven't met many, despite them being out for three years. They still mostly keep to themselves, although things are less frosty between humans and monsters than they were at first.

Maurice hands me my drink and I take a sip, letting the slight warmth from the alcohol thaw out my nerves.

Sofia hops up onto a high stool by the bar. She's a lot shorter than my five foot six, and she really has to hop! "So what are you looking for, Jessie?"

I shrug. "Work. I'll take anything, really."

She shakes her head. "No, but what are you really looking for? If you could dream up a perfect client, who would it be?"

I take another sip of my drink. I'm not even sure I see the point in playing this game, but whatever. I don't want to put her off. So I swirl the pink liquid in the glass and think for a minute. "I guess he'd be big and strong, and really sweet to me." I smile into the drink. "I don't really care what he looks like as long as he treats me well, you know? Like deep down, he's just a nice guy."

Maurice leans across the bar with a wink. "You know, if it's golden retriever energy you're looking for, love, you know which monsters do that best."

Sofia wags a finger at him. "Uh, uh. She's not yours, Rice. There's someone coming for her tonight. I just can't get a good sense of who. Strange."

Coming for me? Um, that sounds sinister.

Before I can question Sofia further, a dark voice from behind makes us turn. "Pardon me, but I do believe this is the very woman I came here looking for."

I stare at Sofia for a moment. I'll be a lot less quick to judge the next time someone says they have any kind of powers, that's for sure.

The owner of the dark voice moves into my line of vision and I have to fight back a sense of disappointment. Not that I was picturing someone in particular, but if I was, it wouldn't be him. He's tall and well built, sure. But not the big beefy guy I had let myself imagine. This guy also looks so put together. His immaculately tailored chinos are rolled at the cuff, revealing expensive looking leather shoes. He's wearing a white business shirt rolled up at the sleeves and unbuttoned at the front to reveal just a hint of muscled chest and a flash of gold chain around his neck. His dark hair is neatly styled and sits a little below his ears. His smile looks positively dangerous.

"Miss Jessie." He offers me his hand and I shake it, but withdraw my hand away as soon as I can.

Sofia smiles. "This is Sethos Issa. He's actually the client who booked you a few nights ago."

My eyes widen and I look at Sethos with fresh eyes. At least I know he's reliable. The job the other night wasn't that bad. Still, if he's come looking for me in person, does that mean he wants more? I'm not sure I want to offer more to him.

Sethos gives me a smile that doesn't quite reach his eyes. "I don't want to give you the wrong impression, Jessie. I'm not looking for myself. I'm booking you for... a friend."

Sofia tips her head to the side and her eyes narrow. "What friend? You know that's against our policy, Mr. Issa."

Sethos holds up his hands defensively. "I read your policies very carefully. All I want is for Jessie to dance at a set time in a set location. I'll have security on site to make sure she's safe."

I tap my nails against my glass. "Just like I did the other night?"

He nods. "Just like that. Slightly different location. I promise you'll be completely safe. I'm happy to up the payment and lock in a week of performances up front. What do you say?"

23

I look back at Sofia who is still regarding Sethos with a hard stare. She glances at me. "What do you think, Jessie? You don't have to answer straight away either."

I shrug. "It felt fine the other night, and I do want more work."

"Perfect." Sethos smiles as if it's settled. "I already sent through a booking request. Can I expect you at nine tomorrow night?"

Sofia cuts in before I can answer. "She'll accept or deny the booking request through the app as usual. I'm going to make sure both parties have signed the full contract and if anything looks off, I'll be calling our security team."

Sethos smirks. "Of course. I'm sure you take great care of your workers. Rest assured I've thought of everything."

A quick nod to Sofia and me, then he turns and slinks back across the bar to the exit.

Sofia's hand on my arm draws my attention back to her. "You don't have to agree to this if it's not what you want, Jessie."

I smile. I'm probably half faking it. There's something I don't like about Sethos, but not enough to put me off. "I'm fine. Really. And thank you."

Sofia waves over Maurice. "I think we need another round here."

But I shake my head. "Nah. It's OK. Thanks."

He leans on the bar and his look turns serious. "Don't ever feel like you have to, yeah? And don't feel ashamed if you have to use the emergency contact number. It'd be my pleasure to come and deal with anyone who tries to give you grief. You hear?"

Is it strange that these two almost feel like friends, although I've only just met them? If only everyone I've met so far in Heartstone was this awesome.

Sofia gives my arm a final pat. "I still have a good feeling for you. Sethos definitely isn't the one, but there is someone. And you'll meet him soon."

FIVE

GIVEN TO THE GARGOYLE

Jessie

I glance down at the instructions Sethos sent me again.

ArtfulMind: Use the back stairs to climb to the east tower. Go ahead and play music and wear whatever you like. Dance for at least fifteen minutes. After that you're free to go.

OK then.

I find the back stair. The door isn't locked, so I push it open and climb up, exiting the staircase at the top. The wind blows my hair in my face as I open the door and lifts the hem of my jacket a little, sending a chill over my bare legs. It's going to be a cold one, dancing up here in lingerie, but I'll warm up with my movements, I hope.

The rooftop is just below the level where I'm standing. I figure that's where he wants me to dance. Maybe he's trying to pull some kind of stunt to get people interested in his theater again. Who knows? I have heard there are no shows on at the Grand these days. Which is a shame. It used to be the biggest theater in Heartstone. I've always dreamed of being in a show at centerstage. How ironic I got booked for one, but with no audience.

To get down to the roof, I'll need to climb down. Hanging out the archway I'm about to climb through is the most lifelike statue I've ever seen. He's perched on a stone pedestal, leaning forward as if he's looking through. His hand on one side of the archway grips it tight. The claws really look as if they're digging into the stone. I stare, fixated by the level of detail in a piece of art you could barely see from the street. The gargoyle appears mostly human. His large frame is hunched over, highlighting the bulging muscles of his broad shoulders and back. Large bat-like wings sprout from his shoulder blades and a long tail curls around the edge of the archway.

His face is what really captures my attention though. He has a strong nose and a burly chin. It's a face that says there are burdens on his wide shoulders. Across the right side of his face cracks run like scars. They crisscross over his body down to his chiseled abdomen and over his right side.

I wonder what his story is. Or was. Or whatever.

Probably just the tortured dream of some medieval sculptor wanting his paycheck.

Tearing my gaze away from the statue, I refocus. I slide my legs over the ledge. Then I grip his tail and slide down to the roof. Everything goes much the same as the last time I was here. I set up a track on my phone and move to the music. My fingers play at the buttons of my jacket. I'm a little slower to undress this time, waiting until my movements warm my body from within, so the icy wind doesn't chill me as much.

It's crazy, but as I dance, my gaze is continually drawn back to the face of the statue. He's my only audience. No one on the street is paying me any attention.

Maybe I'm crazy, but that gargoyle really looks like he's watching me. His head seems to be tilted at a different angle than it was before. Yep. I must be going crazy. Still, what's crazier than a job where I strip on a rooftop where no one will see? I shrug off the creepy thoughts and continue dancing, running my hands over my body, swaying my hips, and losing myself in the music.

When I finish, my breath is coming fast and my body feels alive with energy. I still see no trace of anyone, but I collect my phone and switch off the music. Walking back to the archway,

I grab the gargoyle's tail and haul myself up and back into the tower. Thank God, it's warmer in here.

"Hope you liked the show," I say to my silent observer and give him a pat on his stony arm.

He, of course, says nothing.

I tuck my knees up into my jacket and look down at the city lights. "You sure are a shit tipper, you know that?"

I'm reluctant to go back to the hostel. All that awaits me there are unpleasant smells and unwelcome noise. So I sit a while with my silent friend. I look up at the sky, but of course, it's the dim, dirty black you get in Heartstone.

"You can't even see the stars here," I say after a few minutes. "The city lights are too bright. Back home I'd see them, though. Doesn't matter, I guess. They'd all look different over this side of the world."

I tuck my chin on my knees, thinking about how pathetic it is to sit here talking to a statue like he can hear me. I should get out more. Try to make some friends. I've just been too busy. When the girls in my dorm ask me to come drinking with them, I always say no. Too awkward. I don't want to be locked in if there's someone annoying and then have to come home to her as well.

I sigh. "You're easy company," I tell my friend. At least there are no awkward silences when you're talking to a statue. I can say whatever I want and he won't judge me.

I glance around at him. This time I'm sure his head has moved. It has to have. Before, it looked as if he was looking down at me through the archway. Now it's definitely twisted, so his eyes are once again on me where I sit beside him.

Oh hell no! I saw that episode of Doctor Who. I want the fuck out of here. Now!

Scrambling back from the ledge, I keep my eyes on the gargoyle, fumbling at my pocket to make sure my phone and keys are there. He isn't moving. At least his face still has the same pensive expression. No bared crazy-ass teeth. No snarl. I get to my feet and stagger back, reaching to find the door behind me with a trembling hand.

For one awful moment, I can't turn the knob. My palms are sweaty despite the chill in the air. Then I grip it more tightly. It turns and I escape into the stairway, slamming the door behind me.

I take my life in my hands running down those stairs with six inch heels but I do not care. Better than staying in a spooky haunted tower with a statue that's about to come alive and eat me.

It's only when I make it back to the street, the emergency exit door shutting behind me with a boom, that I remember Monstrous Deals' safety information and Maurice saying to call if anything felt off. Pulling out my phone from my pocket, I bring up the app and find the number. Then I pause.

I'm being ridiculous, aren't I? Nothing happened. I'm on the street under the bright street lights with people going backward and forward about their business. I can't even be sure the statue moved at all. In fact, of course it didn't. I just sat up there too long by myself in the dark and let creepy thoughts make me freak out.

I shake my head.

Putting my phone back in my pocket, I head toward the subway station. I'm glad I didn't call the number. At least no one else has to know what an idiot I am. Though I'm not excited about coming back here tomorrow night. In fact, I think I feel a sore throat coming on. It's just a tickle, but it's definitely the sort of thing that gets worse overnight. I should probably take it easy and make sure it doesn't turn into a full blown cold.

I tell myself I'm not being a coward all the way back to the hostel and as I tuck myself into my tiny bunk. When I close my eyes, it's the stone face of the gargoyle I see behind my eyelids, though. I spend the night restless, waking between fitful bouts of sleep.

SIX

Jessie

I wake the next morning to a crash and the sound of cursing. When I peek through the curtain surrounding my bunk, I see Rachel, the girl from the bunk above mine, has fallen out of bed!

"What the hell? Are you alright?" I poke my head out and look down at her sprawled on the ground below me.

She groans. "I fucking hate this place."

I laugh. I shouldn't. She's probably just hurt herself pretty bad and a moment ago I was annoyed at being woken, but it's just such an irony for her to say that to me.

Rachel stares at me.

"I'm sorry," I say, trying and failing to hold in more laughter. "It's just that I feel exactly the same."

She giggles. Then she starts laughing, too.

She staggers to her feet, rubbing her ass and still giggling. "I should have ended my holiday at the last stop. I'm so over it. I tried to tell myself I should be taking advantage of my last month off, but the truth is I miss home."

I smile. "That's nice, though. Having a home you miss. It'll feel good when you get back."

She nods. "Yeah. It will. You're not missing home?"

I shrug. "I'm not traveling. I've come here to live. I just need to find a job. And an apartment, so I can get out of this place."

"I hear you," she says. "I didn't have enough left to get a private room, but these shared dorms do my head in."

I snort-laugh and immediately regret it when Rachel gives me a quizzical look. "What?"

"Well, it's just... You snore pretty loud, you know."

She winces. "Yeah, sorry about that. Big adenoids. Shoulda had 'em out as a kid, but money was always tight."

"Not your fault, I guess." It's kinda hard to stay mad when she's so reasonable.

"Besides, I think you'll find I'm not the only one who's a noisy sleeper."

I blink up at her. "What do you mean?"

"I mean you were talking in your sleep something fierce last night. Something about some statue coming to life. Scared the crap outta me."

I laugh again. What else can I do? In the light of day, my fears seem even more ridiculous. Of course, the statue didn't come to life.

"Hey, you wanna come get some breakfast with me?" Rachel asks.

I smile. "Sure." I can't think of a reason to refuse and to be honest, she's being so nice it makes me feel like a bit of a dick for all the times I lay here in the dark hating her.

We end up going down to the cheap-ass hostel cafe for a big plate of scrambled eggs and bacon. I drink more coffee than I should and listen to Rachel tell me all about her family. She has five sisters and brothers, the result of a blended family. Sounds like they all get on, too, which I can't even imagine. Back home it's just me and my parents and even before I left, we hardly spoke.

Rachel flips her wavy brown hair back from her face and gives me a smile that wrinkles her freckled nose. "What about you? Why'd you come to Heartstone?"

I sigh. "I just wanted to get away, I suppose. I always dreamed of acting." I hold up my hands. "And I know, it's probably just wishful thinking. That's what my parents always said. They wanted me to go to uni or get an apprenticeship. I went to NIDA instead. That's an acting school in Sydney. That was the beginning of the end."

"And you don't talk to them anymore?"

I shake my head. "Not anymore. Not since I left. We never really saw eye to eye."

"No? They didn't want you acting?"

My lips twist into a wry expression. "They had more of a problem with my other work."

Rachel frowns. "Why? What do you do?"

I don't say anything for a long moment, weighing up whether to say. Some people don't react well. Then again, I might never see her again and she seems like the open-minded sort. "I'm a dancer."

Her eyes widen a fraction. "A danc—oh! A dancer. I take it they're not OK with that."

I shake my head. "When I was still at home, they organized this big intervention at their church. Invited me in so all the elders could tell me how I needed to rejoin the congregation and stop embarrassing my parents. I haven't been since I was twelve! And I'm going to go back to stop my parents from losing face?" I snort. "Not likely. I didn't even stay long enough for them to tell me I was going to hell for showing strange men my tits."

Rachel snorts. "They can keep their judgment to themselves."

"It's not like I want to do it forever. It just pays the bills better than anything else, you know?"

She nods.

"So here I am, hoping to make it for real on the stage."

"I hope you make it, then. Have you got anything lined up?"

"No." I look down at the dregs of my coffee in my cup. "I haven't had a call back from any of the auditions I've attended."

Unexpectedly, Rachel reaches across the table to squeeze my hand. "Hey. Don't give up, OK? You'll find something. You just gotta believe in yourself."

I nod, not trusting myself to talk around the lump in my throat. I should never have assumed she was a horrible person just because she's annoying to live with. Of all people, I should know better than to judge a book by its cover.

"Good on you for leaving behind the negative influences in your life and taking a chance," Rachel says. "I'm sure if you just stay positive, you'll figure something out. Anything is better than being in a situation that's making you unhappy, right?"

"Yeah." She's right. I'm still better off here. It's a good reminder.

Rachel leaves to do some sightseeing, but I sit in the cafe, nurse my cold coffee, and think. I need to make this work. I'm not going to let my crazy imagination stop me from making the most of the opportunity I've been given for work.

In fact, I wonder if there's anything else I can make out of this. This Sethos guy has to be pretty rich to be booking workers for a 'friend' through Monstrous Deals. As far as I know their prices are way higher than normal escort services.

When I google him, I can't believe my eyes. Turns out he owns the Grand Theater, the sports stadium, and two huge shopping malls. That's only in Heartstone. Wikipedia reveals he owns entertainment and retail venues all over the country.

I mean he's got his own wiki page for Christ's sake! OK, I am absolutely going to leverage this to get me somewhere. I just have to figure out how. But it starts with not disappointing him.

I spend the rest of the day psyching myself into performing, telling myself I'm not scared. Not at all.

I do add the Monstrous Deals emergency number to my contacts list and put some pepper spray in my pocket, but that's just taking precautions, right? Doesn't mean I'm scared.

I also make a new playlist and consider buying a new pair of gorgeous pink heels. Then I tell myself to save that cash until I've made my big break. I just need to be super sexy, figure out where Sethos hides himself to watch me, and work out exactly what it is he's looking for.

I'm so totally not scared that the minute I'm up the stairs and into the tower, I walk right up to that gargoyle and pat him on the shoulder. "Bet you thought you'd scared me off, huh?"

I give the statue a confident smile I don't feel. "Well, too bad. I don't scare that easy."

He says nothing, of course. I don't know what I thought I saw last night, but he is facing forward, looking down through the archway toward the glass dome in the center of the roof.

Shaking off the nagging fear that still hasn't stopped creeping up the back of my neck, I pull out my phone and start my new playlist. I put it down on the ledge of the arch and think for a moment. I don't want to just do the same thing I did last night or the first night I came. I have a few routines, but without a new outfit and with no props, one dance could easily look much like another. If I had a pole, there's so much more I could do, but there's nothing here even remotely usable that way.

Back at the club I used to work in, I might choose a patron and offer a free lapdance to get things moving. I look over at my big stony friend. He's hunched forward in a position that would make it awkward, but at least he can't get handsy. By the time my first song is wrapping up, I've decided.

I strip off my jacket and toss it into a corner, making a few strides around the tower while I pick up the beat of the new song. I strut over to the gargoyle with my best fuck me eyes and run my hand from his shoulder and right down his arm. I continue the movement and lower my body into a squat all the way down to the ground. Then, popping out my butt, I lift up again, rolling my body in a sensual movement that never fails to get attention.

No one is here to give me attention, but at least I'm starting to feel good. I've finally shaken the awful feeling dogging me all day, and I'm starting to get into the swing of it.

I put my arms around the gargoyle's neck and move my hips so I'm grinding against him. Then I turn, undo my bra and discard it, covering my breasts with my hands until I turn to face him again. This would be more fun with a live person who'd be giving me a reaction by now. Still, I hold onto him and let my head fall back as I circle around and come back up again. Then I go in for the kill. Facing away and tucking myself between his thighs, I bend all the way forward. This move pushes my ass right against the guy's crotch and I can usually tell how well I've worked the room by what I feel here. Of course, my stone friend is rock hard already. And large. Very large!

That's all I have time to take in before I realize I've miscalculated.

The statue is perched at the opening of the archway and to get into his lap, I precariously positioned myself right on the lip. Leaning forward would overbalance me, but I can't take a step forward to correct. In front of me is only air.

I'm falling head first toward the roof like I've taken a dive. A strong, cold pair of hands grasps my hips, hauling me back against a big body that, while hard, is most definitely *not* stone.

SEVEN

GIVEN TO THE GARGOYLE

William

She almost tips over the edge of my alcove and head first onto the roof below. I reach out before I even realize I can do it, my limbs acting without my conscious direction. Then my hands are at her hips and I am pulling her back against me, wondering if I'll ever be able to let her go.

The way she reeked of fear the other night I thought I'd never see her again. I wanted so badly to say something. To tell her that it was alright. My damn jaw wouldn't unlock, though, so I was trapped in the prison of my stone form as she ran from me. Now she's back and my hands are full of her perfect curves and I think I've died and gone to heaven. Only I know that can't be true, because the only place a sinner like me ends up is hell.

She's soft. So soft and warm, she smells like the most luscious flower that ever bloomed. Her skin is supple under my grip and I'm terrified at any moment my sharp claws will pierce her flesh.

The woman screams and struggles in my hold. I try to turn, to step off my perch, but my feet are still stone. "Please don't be scared." My voice is rough after so long. I have to clear my throat. "Please don't be scared. I only want to keep you safe."

She twists and I spin her carefully around to face me, still holding her nearly naked body so she doesn't fall. She tilts her head back to stare up at me. Her eyes widen, but she doesn't scream again. "Promise?"

"I swear it. I would never harm you." My answer is instant. A gargoyle cannot lie, but these words are the truest I've ever spoken.

"What are you?" She's still staring up at me, but she's not struggling any longer.

Despite my best intentions, my gaze drops to the swell of her lovely breasts for one moment before I wrench my focus back to her face. "A gargoyle." A monster cursed for my sins. I don't say this. No need to give her any more reason to scorn me.

The woman shivers. She must be freezing up here in the chill night air with no clothes on. I've been holding her a little apart from my body to give her some space, but now I tuck her close. I wrap my wings around us both, folding them around her like a cloak.

She gasps, but as soon as she's in my arms, she lays her head against my chest and sighs. "Oh! You're warm now. Before you were cold."

Even my tail curls around her, longing to be allowed contact with this sweet, perfect creature. "I'm not actually made of stone." At least not now. Now that she has reversed the process of petrifaction almost completely in a single night. I'll turn back to stone again in the morning, as I have ever since I was cursed. For now, I'm flesh and blood just like any creature. Well mostly. Except for my feet. Except for the scars that run up and down the right side of my body. My time in the weather has not been kind to me. It didn't bother me until now. Not when I thought I would surrender to it, eventually crumbling to dust. Now, I wonder exactly how hideous she finds me.

The woman gives a little cough. "Well, this is certainly an interesting way to meet. I hope I wasn't interrupting your sleep or something."

I laugh. "Look at you. Princess like you could interrupt me any damn night and I'd be lucky. But no. Gargoyles sleep during the daylight hours."

She hasn't pushed away from me or struggled to be released. In less than half a minute, she's speaking to me as if this is the most natural thing in the world. Damn well feels like it. I can't think of anything more perfect than having her soft curves pressed up against me and breathing in her scent. At my thigh, my cock twitches and yeah, OK, I can imagine one thing that might be more perfect.

That's all it takes. My thoughts stray into dangerous territory and I'm picturing lifting her until she can wrap her legs around my waist, helping her sink down over my cock. God, it's thickening, swelling between us until I'm certain she must feel it, too. I have on only a tiny loincloth. I no longer feel the cold or heat. That means there's nothing to prevent the unruly thing poking her in the belly like some beast.

I should let her go. I really should, but I can't make my body obey. Instead, I pull her closer still and shudder when her softness gives in all the places I'm hard. "What may I call you, princess?" Her name is Jessie, but I can hardly admit I've been leering at her for two nights, now can I?

She smiles up at me and I could swear there's wickedness in the curve of her lips. "Well, I quite like princess, actually. But I suppose you could call me Jessie. If you prefer. What about you? What are you called? Or do gargoyles not have names?"

"We do." Damned if I can remember it right this moment, though. Not with the feel of her up against me racing through every vein in my body, sparking flames. Not with her tucked beneath my wings like she belongs here.

Jessie laughs. "Well, are you going to tell it to me?"

"W-William." By the virgin, I am tripping over my own tongue as if I've never seen a woman before. "William du Buisson, at your service."

She lifts a brow. "Something tells me you really mean that, William. Thank you for saving me by the way."

"It was my pleasure." Lord, was it ever.

She grins, glancing down at the place where her smaller body is pressed against my large hard one. I swallow. I'm so hard, God, she definitely knows. "Yes. So I see. I should probably finish my dance."

"Your dance?"

She nods. "You see, the owner of this theater paid me to come here each night and dance. Only he doesn't watch. At least I think he doesn't. But I'm not sure. So I think I'd better keep dancing if I want to get paid."

I think about letting her. Devil take my soul, I really do. In the end, I find I have a shred of honor left. "It's for me. He's trying to wake me. He told me he'd send you here every night until I woke."

Her eyes widen, but the smile never leaves her face. "Oh! In that case I guess I've done what he paid me for tonight." She pauses and tugs her plump bottom lip between her teeth. "Would you say you're fully woken, though? Because I could really use the pay for the rest of the week, and this is only night two."

A grin stretches over my face when I realize what she's suggesting. "Well in that case, no." I gesture down toward my perch. "Just look at my...feet. They still need some waking. In fact I'm not certain they'll be fully woken for another five nights. Perhaps longer."

She grins back at me "Yeah, that's a real problem. Let me see what I can do about that, then."

Her hand skates down my chest and a tingle spreads through my body. Just before she reaches the place where my loincloth is doing a pathetic job of covering my straining erection, she diverts her touch and leaves me aching. I'm breathless and frozen just as surely as I was while the sun shone full in the sky, waiting with anticipation.

Her smile grows more wicked. "You know, there's an old story about a princess who was poisoned by her evil stepmother and fell into an enchanted sleep so deep everyone thought she was dead. Do gargoyles know human stories?"

I swallow when her fingertips trace up and around my nipples. "We—I used to be human. A long time ago."

Her brow lifts. "Did you?"

I nod. "All gargoyles were human once. Until we were cursed." God, please don't let her ask me about the curse.

Thankfully, she slides both hands up and over my shoulders. "So you know the story?"

I shake my head. "No. I can't say I do, but perhaps it was first told after I was... transformed."

Jessie lifts onto her toes, wraps her arms around my neck and brings my lips close to hers. "Well, in the story, the princess is woken by a prince, who gives her true love's first kiss."

"Uh huh." I can't form words. All that comes out of my mouth is incoherent mumbling. Her red, glossy lips hover so near my own I can practically taste her already.

"I wonder what would happen to a prince who needed to be woken if a princess gave him a kiss."

A soft, mirthless laugh rumbles in my chest. "I'm no prince, Jessie."

All I can see is her smile and the way her perfect white teeth contrast with the bright paint on her lips as she says, "Lucky I'm not really a princess, then."

She presses her lips to mine and, though they only brush mine with the lightest touch, I float in the sensation as if I truly am free from my trap and soaring above the city on outstretched wings.

Too soon she pulls back, sliding her hands down my chest as she lowers to her heels. "That's enough for tonight, though. If I wake you up all at once, then I don't get paid for the rest of the week." She's gone from my arms while I'm still floundering with my stupid racing thoughts.

Bending, she scoops her jacket from the ground and collects the rest of her things. She turns and gives me a wink. "See you tomorrow."

Christ alive! I've never hated my stone perch and the hours of daylight sleep so much in all the years I've been cursed.

EIGHT

William

I twist my body to stare after her as she slips through the door to the stairs and leaves me. I peer over the edge of the building at the street below to catch a glimpse of her as she passes.

I feel a hundred years younger. More! I have movement in limbs I haven't moved in years and an ache in my stiff cock, which still hasn't calmed since holding her in my arms. It's hard to believe my body reacted so powerfully to this little human. I have no doubt if she returns she'll be able to rouse me fully. Then it dawns on me: there's only one reason for me to respond so powerfully to her.

Gargoyle legend isn't well known. As a rule, gargoyles are not creatures who seek the company of others. For one reason or another, many of us tend to live alone, hardly ever meeting to talk to others of our kind. So I'm a little vague on the details. But I've heard stories of a fated mate who is a gargoyle's only hope of ever breaking their curse. A fated mate who is damn near irresistible.

Beneath my loincloth, my dick gives a little jump. Would I be able to resist if she comes back to dance naked in front of me, to rub those enticing curves up against my newly woken flesh and press those sweet lips against mine?

Not a chance! If I get her back in my arms again, I'm not sure I'd ever be able to let her go. I don't even need the added temptation of breaking the curse. Her allure is enough. But if I take her, she'll be bound to me forever.

Jessie is bright and beautiful as the first flower of spring. And far less delicate. I'd happily follow her around, regardless of a bond. If I wasn't tethered in place, I'd be on that street following her home right now! Yet, I hesitate. She doesn't need to be saddled with a great cumbersome beast like me.

With a start, I realize what I must do.

I must pretend I'm not interested in her dances. I'll have to shut my eyes and shut off my senses from her to give me the strength of will to send her away. She doesn't deserve to be held back. Not by me.

That sounds like the worst form of torture I've endured in nearly one thousand years. But for her, I'll do it. I'll do anything.

The thought throws me into a foul temper and I hunch, glaring across the city without seeing anything but the tantalizing form of my princess dancing for me in my mind's eye.

When Sethos turns up with a big shit-eating grin on his face a little while later, it's all I can do not to wipe it off with my fist. "What do you want?"

He leans against the frame of my archway and looks me up and down. "To see if I got what I paid for yet."

I'm torn. On the one hand, I want nothing more than to have Jessie back here every night for the rest of the week. I want her in my arms again and I want to breathe in her scent and feel her lips against mine. But that's a very bad idea.

Still, she said she needs the money. I don't want to cheat her out of payment.

"Yeah. Worked." I wave my arms around to show Sethos I can.

His grin grows pointy. "Did it, now?"

"Yes. Why don't you pay that girl what you promised her and tell her not to worry about coming back?" I could kick myself. But I'm doing this for her.

Sethos steps closer, prodding me in the chest. "I don't know what game you're playing, William, but a guardian isn't much good to me if he can't move from his pedestal. You think I haven't noticed you can't lift your feet? No. She'll be back here every night for as long as it takes to get what I want. What we both want. I don't know why you've got all sour on her now. Do I need to pay her to do more than dance?"

My jaw nearly hits my stone perch. Pay her for more? To fuck me? "No!" Everything in me rebels against the vision of her spreading her legs for me only because she thought she had to. For money. I don't want her to ever feel she has to do anything she doesn't want. Especially not for me.

"No." I shake my head firmly. "Don't do that. Just get her to come back for one more night, and pay her out for the rest of the week."

I'm sure it won't take more than that to wake up the rest of my body enough for me to move. I can stay strong for one more night.

Sethos shakes his head. "Just don't lie to me, du Buisson. Didn't anyone ever tell you a sphinx can smell a lie from a mile away? Don't waste your breath. Save it to guard my theater."

He turns and stalks down the stairs, leaving me longing for the day I'll be able to chase him down and pound into him the need for him to mind his own fucking business.

If he'd have left well enough alone, my poor lovely human would never have even met me, and I'd never have been any the wiser. I could have succumbed to my end without regret. Now?

GIVEN TO THE GARGOYLE

How can I go back to stone when I know somewhere out there she's breathing the same air as me? Looking so lush and ripe I'd like to pluck her from the tree and sink my teeth in her.

God's blood, I'm in for a world of hurt tomorrow evening. I can't regret the way the conversation went, though.

She's worth it. Seeing her one more time is worth any cost.

NINE

GIVEN TO THE GARGOYLE

Jessie

I take extra care preparing for tonight. It's stupid. It's just a job, after all. Not a date. I keep telling myself this while I shave my legs and my bikini line and my underarms and check at least five times that my hair looks nice and the polish on my toenails isn't chipping.

OK, I'm being ridiculous. He's not going to be looking at my toenails that closely. But I'll know. For some reason, I really want to look my best for this gruff gargoyle who seems to stumble over his words and finds it hard to smile. Maybe it's that he seems to stumble over them especially because I'm around. As if he's so overwhelmed with my presence he can hardly talk.

God, that's flattering. Or it would be, if it was true and not just my imagination.

I choose my newest set of lingerie: pink with black bows and black ribbon trim and my stay-up black tights with my black heels. I even wear a dress, for an extra layer of mystery. I figure if I've only got one person in the audience, I might as well draw out the show for his enjoyment.

So when I climb the stairs and step out into the tower, I'm disappointed when he doesn't even turn.

"Hello." I try to use my best sultry, sexy voice as I saunter up behind William. He doesn't move. He doesn't reply.

I slink around so I can look at him from the side, but he remains locked in place, as still as the first night I danced for him.

Has he turned back to stone? His skin never changed from the marbled gray color it was when I first saw him, not even when he was awake.

Reaching out a tentative hand, I place my fingertips against his bicep. Warm. Subtly soft to the touch, though he is firm in all the right ways. It's not like that first night when I held onto his tail to slide down onto the roof. His body is flesh, not stone. So why is he just standing there? He hasn't even turned his head to look at me. He still stares rigidly out the archway toward the street below the theater.

"Are you ready for me to dance now?"

No response.

Huh. Well I'm not giving up that easy. I flick through my phone and select the song I want. Let's see if he really is just ignoring me.

I begin. Moving away, I slowly undo the jacket with my back to William. When I shrug it off and turn to see his reaction, he still isn't even looking.

I drop the jacket to the ground and stalk over to him. Time to raise the stakes. I use his body, just like I did last time, grinding and dropping low to slide back up again. When I deliberately turn and allow my ass to brush against his arm, I spin to see the muscles in his neck bunched and tighter than they were before and his hands balled into fists. I allow a little smile to curve the corner of my mouth.

Whatever this game, I'm going to win.

Still moving to the music, I consider. I liked kissing him last time. I wouldn't usually kiss a client during a dance. I'm pretty strict about how much touch I allow. But I can't stop thinking about his firm lips against mine and how much I want him to sweep his tongue into my mouth and really kiss me back. I step closer, running my hands up his chest. His hands clamp over my wrists and stop me.

"You should leave." His voice is little more than a growl.

Why do I get the sense he's holding onto his control by a thread? "Why would I leave? I'm paid to dance for you, right? Just making sure you get your money's worth."

"Christ, Jessie. Don't say it like that. It's not even my money. Just go, OK? I'll make sure you get paid."

I step back and he releases me. "Is that what this is about, then?"

A muscle tics in his jaw. "You've done your part. No need to waste more of your time on me."

"Oh really?" I pull my dress slowly over my head, noting the way his gaze drops to rove over my body and he swallows visibly. Those muscles in his neck and shoulders aren't the only thing bulging right now.

I drop the dress to the ground and cup my breasts over the bra. "Why don't you prove that to me? Step off that perch and come over here. Prove you're cured."

"No."

I smirk. "No? You can't, can you?"

"No." The rumble of his growl vibrates through my body, sending shivers down my spine.

"Well then I guess you can't stop me doing whatever I want over here, then. Can you?"

I laugh to myself and tease my nipples through the fabric of my bra until they're stiff peaks. Reaching behind, I unfasten it and drop it to the pile of clothes on the ground.

William lets out an unsteady breath. Does he realize he's turned his head to get a better look at me? I'm not sure.

I don't stop there. I make a little moaning noise as I play with my breasts some more. Lifting and plumping them, I pull at the nipples between my thumb and finger until sensation shoots through me. The little noises I make as I slide my own hands down my belly and into my underwear aren't just for show. I'm excited about the near wild look in his flinty gray eyes and the way his jaw looks like he's grinding his teeth hard enough to crack them.

As soon as my fingertips push over my mound and into my pussy, I feel the slick there and know I'm doing more than teasing him. Unlike William though, I don't intend to hold back. I'm not going to deny myself. So I slide two fingers right over my clit and gasp as pleasure grows.

William's nostrils flare and behind his shoulders, his wings extend to beat the air. "God's troth, woman, you have no idea what you're doing, do you?"

I laugh. "Oh trust me, I've done this a few times before."

He groans when I slide my pink panties over my hips and let them fall to my ankles. Then I step out of them and spread my legs, watching William's mouth drop open and the bulge beneath his tiny loincloth visibly pulses.

"Don't—"

I don't even let him finish his protest before my hand is back at my cunt, sliding through the wetness and drawing circles around my aching, swollen bud.

"Fuck!"

He breathes the curse as I push two fingers inside myself. He can't see everything I'm doing, but the erotic noises I can't help must tell him what he can't make out with vision alone.

I moan as I sink my fingers deep, rocking my palm over my clit, almost coming at the feel of my fingertips against my G-spot.

GIVEN TO THE GARGOYLE

"You either need to stop right the fuck now, or get that pussy over here," William snarls.

I'm almost too lost in the moment to respond. His fierce crude words make me clench around my fingers, driving my pleasure higher.

"Can't stop," I gasp. "Not now." It's true. Something about this escalating tension, about the face off between his desire and whatever else is going on here is making me crazy.

William roars. With another beat of his wings that almost knocks me off my feet, he launches forward off his perch and grabs my hand. I think he's going to stop me. Perhaps manhandle me off his tower and back onto the street. Instead he locks eyes with me and brings my hand to his lips, slowly taking my fingers into his mouth. Then he sucks my slick from my skin, never taking his gaze from mine.

A low growl is the only warning I get that he is far from done.

Suddenly, he releases my wrist, places a hand on each of my hips, and lifts me straight into the air. I squeal at the giddy sensation. I moan when he guides my legs around his ears and brings my pussy directly to his face.

On instinct, I grab at his short horns, holding tight to avoid falling as his mouth latches firmly onto me. The pleasure is immense. It's immediate and consuming, and I'm sure I'm making enough noise people on the street will hear. I don't care.

William's hands on my ass keep me firmly in place. He rumbles approval when I tighten my grip with hands and thighs. Then he devours my pussy so thoroughly I don't think I'll ever be the same.

57

My god, the way his tongue spears inside me I have to wonder if it's normal-sized. Perhaps it's not. I swear he reaches places inside me I'm not even sure have been reached by a cock or my dildo before. Then he plants his mouth over my clit and suckles.

I come, shuddering and moaning uncontrollably. I fall into his arms, still twitching from the most intense orgasm of my life. It takes me a moment to realize this very big, very strong gargoyle is now looking at me as if I'm his favorite meal and his worst enemy wrapped up in one. "You don't know what you've done."

I shiver, both from the aftershocks of what he just did to me, and his words. When I can catch my breath, I say, "I don't know what you mean. Pretty sure you're the one who just wrecked me."

He growls again and the grin dies on my lips. "You don't know, do you?" Ice and fire fills his tone, yet when he sets me down, he does it carefully, as if I'm made of china. I stand on shaky feet.

"Just go." His voice is raw and clipped. He's turned away from me.

I plant my hands on my hips. "Tell me."

"Just go!" He rounds on me, spreading his wings to seem ten times as large.

I cower.

"Go. And don't fucking come back here, you understand?"

I nod. "O-OK. I'm going."

William hunches forward, head in his hands as his body is wracked by some seizure. I hesitate.

"Go!"

GIVEN TO THE GARGOYLE

Snatching up my things, I rush into the stairwell, fumbling with my clothes and almost tripping on the stairs just like the night I ran from him. Only tonight when I go, it's not fear. Not really. I mean I feel a little scared of the wild beast-like fury in his eyes when he roared at me. But I also feel an aching emptiness at the pain that so obviously clings to him. After the way he made me feel, I'd like nothing better than to help him feel good, too. Whatever that takes. But he doesn't want me. He doesn't want me anywhere near him. I haven't felt that kind of stinging rejection since my parents told me I wasn't welcome in their home any longer.

TEN

GIVEN TO THE GARGOYLE

William

Jessie runs from me, slamming the door to my tower closed behind her. I grip the edges of my archway and roar my frustration to the night sky. I know with absolute certainty I've just made the second biggest mistake of my life.

I pace the tower, body taut with frustration. When I can't take it any longer, I launch myself to the roof and fling myself over the side, stretching my wings wide for the first time in years. The burn on my unused muscles feels good. For a single moment I wonder if my wings will hold me. Wind whistles past my ears and cold air blows in my face. Cracked and ugly as they are though, they do their job. Too soon my claws touch the ground and I breathe in deep, trying to catch her scent.

Nothing.

Ignoring the strange looks of humans I pass, I jog to the corner and try again. The wind changes, lifting the odor of car exhaust and city sewers for a moment and giving me the tiniest hint of sweet currants and earthy spices. *Jessie.*

It doesn't take me long to catch up with her. She glances back and her eyes widen when she catches sight of me. I'm not sure what reaction I expect. I don't know why I'm surprised when a look of horror crosses her face and she breaks into a jog.

I'm sure I look even more monstrous than usual. My harsh, cracked features, my hideous wings and claws and tail would be enough to make any human run from me, let alone my snarling face.

Unfortunately when she runs from me, it only makes me more desperate to catch her. "Jessie! Wait!" My bellow draws more looks from other humans in the street.

An older woman in a gray coat gasps and several people cross the street to get out of my way. Good. The fewer bodies in my way, the better.

Jessie glances back again, colliding with a man in a dark suit holding a cell phone to his ear. He drops the phone with a curse, grabbing Jessie's arm roughly. "Hey!"

Jessie pulls out of his grip, but I'm already closing the distance.

There is no excuse for his hands on her. The asshole is already snatching up his phone and beginning to walk away as if he doesn't realize he's just committed a fatal error.

With a roar, I double my speed and cut him off. I'm taller anyway, but I stretch to my full height, spread my wings and snarl in his face. "How dare you fucking touch her!"

The guy reels back for a moment, glaring at me. "Damn monsters. This city's a bloody rats' warren these days." He thrusts a finger in my face and it takes everything in me not to grab it and snap it off. "You don't scare me, asshole. I know the terms of the treaty. Monster-human violence isn't tolerated."

I step forward until his finger is pressing against the center of my chest. Then I step forward again until it bends. I give him a grin that is anything but friendly. "They'll have to find what's left of you first."

"William!" Jessie pushes between us. Her soft palms sliding over up the muscles of my chest instantly cool my anger. I'm about to let her push me away from him, when the guy holds up his phone and she looks back.

"Hey, did you just take a picture?"

He smirks. "Oh, you don't want the world to know what a filthy little monster fucker you are, huh? Should have thought about that before you spread your legs, sweetheart."

Jessie's hands lift from me. With a speed greater than I imagined possible, she darts forward and snatches the tiny device. Then she smashes it to the pavement.

"Oh, you little bitch." The asshole lunges for her, but I'm too fast for him. I pull Jessie against my chest with one arm and spin so she's tucked behind me. With the other, I grab him by his neck and fling him backward. He lands on his ass in a puddle, but I don't stop to enjoy the look on his face. I can't stop. If I look at him again, I'll tear him apart.

Instead, I scoop Jessie into my arms and take off. She gasps and wraps her arms around my neck, but she doesn't scream. Perhaps she's too scared.

As soon as I gain some height, I scan for a place to roost. Instinct drives me to take her back to my tower, where my perch calls me to return. But that's not a suitable place for a soft little human like my pretty Jessie. So I turn away from the Grand Theater and fly instead for the nearest high-rise buildings, squinting through windows until I spot what I'm looking for. It's cold. She buries her face in my neck to keep out of the cutting wind. I hate knowing her perfect skin is reddening as I fly.

When I find what I'm looking for, I twist in the air. At the last minute I fold my wings, tuck Jessie tightly against me, and dive through the large glass window on an apartment, feet first with an enormous crash. Shattered glass spews ahead of me into the apartment and over the floor. It's not tough enough to penetrate my hide, but it would tear up Jessie's delicate feet.

Instead of setting Jessie down, I carry her through the living room looking for a bedroom. A high pitched wail emanating from a box by the front door makes me want to claw off my ears. I put my fist through the box and part way into the wall on the other side, which silences the noise.

Good.

I continue my search.

Two doors down a dimly lit corridor, I spot a bedroom. A large soft-looking bed is pushed against a wall where an enormous painting with jagged golden lines hangs. This is more like what my princess deserves.

The far wall is all glass with a window seat where plush cushions are artfully arranged, and a fluffy white blanket is folded over the edge. Setting down Jessie, I collect the blanket and drape it over her bare legs. She's shivering. The night is cold and flying is always colder. I didn't have her in the air long, but it was still too long.

Fuck!

She tucks her feet up on the end of the bed and pulls the blanket higher. "Thanks."

I sigh. "You shouldn't thank me."

The little woman fixes me with a stern look. "William, you just saved me from getting beat up by that guy on the street back there."

I hang my head. "You mean I chased you down and humiliated you. I heard what he called you."

She scowls. "That prick had no right to say that shit."

When I look up again, that fierce look has ignited, but this time I don't get the impression it's directed at me. I don't know what to say, though. I *am* a monster. No question. She could do far better than to get involved with me. That's the whole reason I chased her off my tower. I should have never got off my perch. I should have never allowed myself to put my hands on her.

Now with the trace of her luscious scent hanging around my face, I can't seem to think about anything else.

"Say something." Her voice sounds thin, as if her resolve might crack any moment.

I search her face, but I can't decipher what she's looking for. "He had no right to put his hands on you, either. To look at you. To breathe the same fucking air!"

She laughs, and something hard and gnarly in my chest crumbles a little. "That's exactly the right thing to say."

Moments later though, her chin wobbles and I see tears clinging to her dark lashes. I'm on my knees in front of her in a heartbeat. "Hey, don't cry. Are you hurt? Were you cut coming through the window?" I tug at the blanket trying to search every inch of exposed skin beneath it, but her small hand over mine makes me freeze.

"Not hurt. Just glad you don't hate me."

I stare at her. "*Me*? Hate *you*?" I can hardly process the thought.

She sniffs, still not letting go of my hand.

Very carefully, cautious not to startle her, I let it rest on her knee. She stays where she is and my hand is allowed to remain touching its little piece of heaven.

"I could never hate you, princess. I'm sorry for making you think that. Truly."

"Then what happened back at the theater?"

I sigh. It's clear I'll have to tell her at least part of the truth. I wonder how much I can get away with leaving out. "I don't want you to get... tied up with a beast like me," I say finally.

She snorts, and I'm amazed again at how she goes so swiftly from crying to laughing. "What? You think you got a magic dick or something? Like I'll get addicted?"

I grunt. "Of course not..." I clear my throat. "It is very hard, though. What with being made of stone."

She narrows her eyes at me. "Did you just make a joke?"

I shrug. "That bad huh?"

She smiles at me. "OK, but this ain't my first rodeo. I've given private lap dances before and managed not to get *tied up*," she lisfts up on her elbows to cock an eyebrow at me. "I've fucked guys, and there's no ring on this finger."

I scrub my hand over my face. Just the thought of her fucking other guys does nasty things to my insides. The thought of her giving lap dances to other guys has me itching to punch something. The only thing stopping me from tearing apart the room is the thought of her dancing in *my* lap. So I hang on to that. I sit with my back against the foot of the bed and shake my head.

A few moments later, the corner of the blanket tickles my arm and a shapely calf slips one to either side of me. Jessie's small, cool fingertips smooth over my brow. "That bothers you, doesn't it?"

"No." I'm scowling more than ever. What right do I have to be bothered by what she does? She'd never accept me. She can never be *mine*.

"It does!" She comes around to stand in front of me and I have to avert my eyes. The jacket is gone again and her tantalizing body is on display save for a few scraps of fabric. God, the witchcraft of modern underwear. It doesn't matter how many times I see it, it always casts a spell on me. It's nothing compared to the spell cast by her pure, naked form, though. Jessie slips the bra off. I know because it drops to the floor on the exact spot on the carpet where I'm rigidly fixing my gaze. I groan.

"How long do you think we have before the owners get home?" she asks.

I inhale, then let out a long shaky breath. "The scents in this apartment are old. They haven't been here for weeks. Perhaps months."

"Huh." The panties join the bra on the floor and I swallow.

"Why are you doing this? You don't have to."

Two small hands clasp my cheeks and direct my face until I'm looking up at her. Sweet Christ, she is just as stunning as I remember. My eyes don't know which curve to trace.

"I know, but I want to, OK? Because I can't offer everything to you and have you look at me like you did in that tower."

I stare at her, to shocked to speak. When I finally find my voice, it's rough as hell. "Look at you like what?"

"Like you didn't want me anywhere near you."

"Fuck, Jessie—"

She puts her hand over my mouth. "Just don't say anything. Can you just let me do this?"

Holy fucking Christ! I'd be mad not to.

ELEVEN

GIVEN TO THE GARGOYLE

Jessie

Why do I do these things? I'll probably only feel it harder when I finish and he sends me away again. I just hate being told no. I hate offering myself and being rejected. I've had more than my fair share of entanglements with clients. Each time, I thought they wanted more than just to get in my pants. I thought they really cared about me. Turned out I was wrong. Or they couldn't look past the fact I wasn't going to quit stripping just because I was boning them.

Something about William's hands shaking as they run over my skin and the intense look in his dark eyes has me hoping this is something else, though. That he's different from those other guys.

So, I climb into his lap and break all the rules, just like I did earlier when he lifted my pussy to his mouth and ate me out. I'm not really sure anymore what this is. All I know is I'm desperate to blow his mind. Desperate to make him feel even a little of the things I felt when he held me in his arms like I weigh nothing and sent me soaring into the best orgasm of my life, toys included.

His arms go around me instantly, hands drifting from my hips to my waist and back again, as if he's not sure where to put them. I reach back and guide them to my ass. He groans. Between my thighs, trapped between us, his cock pulses.

I know he's not immune to the things I'm feeling. Clearly he's affected, too. For some reason, he's been trying to resist. That does all sorts of things to me. Usually, it's me trying to set some boundaries. Trying to keep the guy's hands off me. Does it make me an asshole that I want to wear him down until he gives in?

Normally in this position, my breasts would be in the guy's face and I'd just grind against him for a while, take off my bra, and give him a good show. With William, our size difference is so large he'll have to actually bend his head to get to my breasts. That doesn't stop me reaching behind me and unhooking my bra, slipping one strap over each arm at a time. When I pull away the lacy fabric, my nipples are already pebbled into tight buds. Strong hands dig into my ass, increasing the friction where our bodies meet. His hot breath huffs against my skin. I gasp into his mouth when he claims my lips in a punishing kiss.

It's firm and commanding, but with just the right amount of give as he slides his tongue against mine. It's clear he has experience, so what is making him hold back?

When I push my hands into his hair and take hold of his horns, he lets me guide his mouth to my breasts. They're aching for his touch, so the suction as he closes his lips around my nipple has me moaning.

No part of this is a performance anymore. It's no longer just about making him want me, either. Right now, it's pure desire. My core throbs with need and my panties are a mess. I roll my hips to give myself some relief, but only make it worse. I feel like I'm quickly losing whatever control I had over this situation, but since he's still not actually fucking me, William still has far too much.

Time to up the ante.

Lifting myself off his lap should probably earn me some kind of medal. It takes all the willpower I have. I do it though, determined to bring my A game. William lets me go, but the bulge between his spread thighs and the dazed look on his face is gratifying. He presses his eyes closed for a moment and I can see the strain in his furrowed brows and tense jaw. "You're right. We should stop."

I shake my head. "I'm not ready to stop."

I'm not. I want to uncover him. To see what he looks like. I want to trace the length of him and watch his body's reaction to me. I want to make him curse and groan and dig his hands into my flesh again. I want to feel him come undone and lose the stony restraint walling him off from me.

His hand lifts to caress my leg and drifts higher until his thick fingers are teasing at the place my thigh meets my ass. "Jessie, you don't know what you're asking for."

I smile down at him. "Let me make you come like you made me. Is that clear enough for you?"

His throat bobs as he swallows. He doesn't stop me though. I get to my knees in front of him and carefully pull aside the fabric of his loincloth to reveal his swollen erection.

His cock juts up toward me, thick and veiny, looking absolutely delicious. Already moisture beads at the tip. William sucks in a sharp breath when I swirl my thumb through it, slicking the pad around his cockhead. Oh, I could play with him for such a long time. I love the feel of his thick length in my hand. It's weighty and hot, and it pulses for me every time I flick my eyes up to his or lick my lips. So, I toy with him for a while, stroking leisurely up and down, loving the way his eyelids flutter closed only for him to snap them back open again as if he doesn't want to miss a moment.

Then I lean down and take him into my mouth and moan at the flavor. He's salty, of course. Beneath that he's earthy and rich. I'm a little surprised at myself. Not that I dislike the act.

Not at all, but I've never done it just because I liked the way someone tasted before.

I'd do that for him.

I slide off him so I can lap at the moisture on the tip before I take him in my hand and really concentrate on making it good. William groans when I take him deep. So I guide his hand to my head and almost melt from the look in his eyes as I do. There's nothing stony about the heat and desperation there when I look up at him under my lashes. My pussy throbs in time with the way I bob my head. I swear I feel his pleasure like my own.

He lets out a ragged cry. His hand tightens in my hair and then he explodes. I moan when salty liquid fills my mouth, spilling out the corners. I pull back and give him a few final strokes with my hand. The last of his come trickles from the head of his cock and drips over my knuckles.

Then there's a moment. It's probably short, but it feels stretched as if too much is crammed into it. I don't need his words to know something big has happened. Something important. I feel it, too.

Lightly, William's thumb caresses my cheek and brings me back to myself. "My perfect princess. You need to go before I recover and take you despite myself." He shakes his head. "Fuck, the way your mouth feels, I can only imagine what that sweet little pussy would be like around me."

"Look, I want this. You want this. It's fine. You don't have to worry, OK?"

He sighs. "Sweetheart, once I have you, there's no going back. You will be mine. Until I crumble into dust."

I bite down on the inside of my cheek at the sudden rush of tears I refuse to shed. "Y-you don't mean that."

William leans forward, cupping the back of my neck and bringing my forehead to his. "Believe me, Jessie. I can't say anything to you that I do not mean. It's part of the curse." He sighs. "But you don't want that. You're too young and beautiful to give yourself to a creature like me the way I'll take you. You ready to promise me no other man gets to look at you, to *think* about you?"

I open my mouth to answer yes, of course, but I snap it shut again. "My job... I mean you know it's just work, right?"

He shakes his head. "I can't blame you for it, but I couldn't live with it. I'll be a danger to every client you take. And I'm in no position to tell you not to work. I'd support you if I could, but I've got nothing more than the stone perch I rest on each day."

I pull back, pushing my fingers through my hair. Things have gone from one to a hundred very quickly. I can't deny a huge part of me longs for exactly what William is offering. Haven't I wanted all my life to feel what it's like to be loved unconditionally? Irrevocably? He can't mean that, though. No one can love me like that. Not when my own parents can't.

I nod, words sticking in my throat.

William mirrors my movement, lifting himself to his feet and replacing his loincloth. "Thank you for what you did for me tonight. I'll never forget it. But if you don't want to be mine, you have to stay away from now on. Now, I'm free. Because I want you too much to let you go a second time."

A watery smile pushes through the whirlwind of my feelings. "You know that's not as persuasive as you think it is, right now. But I take your point." I get to my feet and find my clothes.

"Come." William holds out his hand for me. "I'll take you home safe. We can't linger here."

TWELVE

William

I remember sleepless nights as a man. I remember tossing and turning on my straw pallet on the ill-fated journey to the Holy Land. Too pent up with excitement and restless energy to sleep.

Sleepless days as a gargoyle are not like that.

They are far, far worse.

As a gargoyle, I'm locked in place. I can't turn my head. I can't move my hand to scratch my balls, let alone pace my tower or swoop down from the roof of the theater to track Jessie's scent back to the awful place she calls home.

It took all my willpower to set her down at the doorway of the inn where she's staying, and smelling the stink of cheap alcohol and vomit. Unwashed sheets and cooking oil, and her despair.

I hate knowing she doesn't want to stay there. She doesn't have to tell me, I could feel it in the way her hands lingered on my arms after I set her down. The way her eyes flicked back to me as she walked through the door.

Most of all, I hate knowing I can't provide a better home for her. There's no question she's my mate. No one else could have reversed the process of petrifaction without me even sinking my cock into her perfect cunny. No one else could rouse the kind of jealous possessiveness I feel even now. Even frozen into stone, my heart burns with the need to have her close, to watch and protect her.

But I'll never see her again. Not if she listens to me. If she knows what's good for her she'll stay away. I'll never get to smell her spicy sweet currant scent again or watch the way her rosy lips part on a sigh when she first runs her fingers through her wet pussy.

Selfish bastard I am, when I wake as night falls across the city, I instantly turn my head to the door of the tower, hoping against hope she'll appear. Christ, let her ignore my thoughtless words. Let her desire for me be halfway as fierce as mine for her, and she'll be back here tonight, unable to help herself.

She doesn't come.

Somehow, I stop myself from leaving my tower in search of her. I dig my claws into the stonework and tear chunks from my archway, but I stop myself.

So when morning breaks and my body turns back to stone, I know I'm in for another awful, sleepless day.

THIRTEEN

Jessie

I hate not dancing for William tonight.

I hate knowing he's waiting there in that tower wondering if I'll come. Wondering if I listened to him but hoping I'll come anyway. At least that's what I think he's thinking. It's what I'd be thinking if I was him.

How can I miss someone I hardly know?

All I know is I spend half my day and night picturing his hands and mouth on me. The other half I spend dreaming of the taste of his cock when I took it into my mouth and the groan he made as he exploded for me.

He's right, though. I can't afford to give up stripping and I know from personal experience it's usually a deal breaker. At least William was honest enough to admit that up front, unlike other guys I've been with.

Sitting with my feet tucked up on my bunk, I eat the last few bites of my sushi dinner and flick listlessly through my phone. My bank balance looks healthier than last week, but I still have to pay for next week's accommodation and food. I'll have to make more if I want to have enough for a security deposit.

I have no new requests on the Monstrous Deals app either. With a sigh, I switch across to Glitterbabes where I take human only bookings. Funny how that's suddenly way less appealing.

A little red dot in my notifications box tells me I've got a new request.

MrHung: Hi gorgeous, you did my brother's bucks party a few weeks ago and I can't stop thinking about your perfect tits. Was hoping I could book you this weekend for a job in the city.

*Getting a few of the boys together. I can pay in advance. Price is
negotiable.*

I sigh. If I remember rightly, this guy was the handsy drunk
at the bachelor party I did three weeks ago, and the reason I
signed up for Monstrous Deals in the first place. The reason
I've been avoiding Glitterbabes. Still the offer of payment in
advance and a negotiable price has me pausing before I hit
delete.

On impulse, I open up a reply.

Jessie: How much are we talking? $500?

I'm just about to shut the app, when a reply pops up.

*MrHung: no problem. 3539 Alba Lane. See you Saturday,
gorgeous girl.*

It's not a question. I also note he hasn't mentioned
anything about pre-payment.

Rolling my eyes I lock my screen and throw my phone
down on the bed. I don't want to deal with this right now. I'll
answer him tomorrow. I should be practicing for the audition
I've got tomorrow. It's a soap commercial. Not my dream job,
but it's not stripping either. It's a step in the right direction.

The icky feeling clings to my skin, though, so I get up and
grab my towel, then head for the shower. When I get back, a
slim girl with long dark hair is throwing her bag up onto the
bunk above mine.

Rachel headed home early after all. Good for her, I guess.
I should be pleased not to have to deal with her snoring any
more. Only after our breakfast the other day, I'm kinda
bummed. Strange that.

I give the new girl a smile I don't feel. "Hi. I'm Jessie."

"Melinda. Nice to meet you."

I make some excuse about having to get up early and scramble into bed, wishing I'd had a chance to say goodbye to Rachel. Heartstone is a lonely city sometimes, despite all the people.

The next day dawns bright and sunny and I'm in a better mood. I scarf down a quick coffee at the hostel cafe and head a few subway stations north to Polbridge, hoping I'll be somewhere close to the beginning of the line.

I'm not though. When I arrive I find a hundred other girls there already. I give my name to the assistant and take a seat on the pavement, giving a grim smile to the chick in front of me. Head down, I go over the lines in my head, picturing how I'll smile; how I'll use my hands.

By the time they call my name, it's almost lunch time. I'm hungry and my ass is numb from sitting on the concrete. Wiping my sweaty hands on my jeans, I put my shoulders back and push open the door. I'm already smiling when my eyes find the faces of the two middle aged women sitting behind the desk.

"Thanks, Jessie. You can begin whenever you're ready."

I take a deep breath. Then I run my hand slowly up my arm, as if I'm lathering. I lift my eyes to the woman closest to me and give her the smile I use to draw a new customer into buying a lap dance. "Some soaps can be harsh on your skin." I sigh, then run my hand back down my arm again before I begin on the other side. "But not Nood. It leaves my skin feeling amazing."

The audition itself takes less than five minutes. I say the lines, they ask a couple of questions, and then I'm dismissed. They don't even ask to see it again. They say nothing about call-backs and how many girls they're going to shortlist.

I smell another failure.

My belly rumbles aggressively. I've got nothing going on now. No work today. Nowhere to be. I sure as hell don't want to go back to the hostel yet. So I grab a hot dog from a cart on the next street. Walking for a while, I look for a bench or a park where I can sit.

Turning the next corner, the elegant curved arches and marble facade of the Grand Theater immediately catch my eye. I hadn't realized I was only a few blocks away. I think of William up on his stone perch, frozen in place in the sun. He said I should stay away because he wouldn't be able to let me go a second time, but surely there's no harm during the day. He's sleeping, right? He probably won't even know I'm there. I'd sure like the company, though. Even if he can't exactly talk to me, there's something reassuring about his quiet, solid presence. Well, there is now I feel like I know him a little. It almost makes me laugh how freaked out I got the night I thought he was a creepy people-eating statue.

When I go to the back door of the theater and enter the access code, the door unlocks and I let myself in. The building is dark, just the strip lighting along the floor and a few emergency lights are on. The tower is windy today, but I tuck my hoodie up over my head and settle in a spot with my back against the arch, looking up at William's frozen face. His jaw looks tight today. Like he was clenching his teeth when he fell asleep. I much preferred the softer look on his face right after I made him come.

The thought makes my pussy give a little flutter. I smile at the memory, completely forgetting my lunch for a moment until my rumbling belly reminds me again.

I sigh. "Think I fucked up another audition," I tell William. William says nothing, of course.

I don't think it's the audition that's really bothering me, though. By now I'm used to failed auditions. You grow thick skin in this industry. Kinda like William, really. I think after a while you either turn to stone or crumble.

"I'm going to have to take a human job this weekend." I scrunch the paper from my lunch in my fist, balling it as tight as I can get it. The corners of the wrapper cut into my palm. "It's good pay."

I imagine William's fierce look of disapproval if he could move. I know he'd see right through me. Some actress!

I try a brighter smile. "It's great pay, actually."

After another long silence, I say, "Only I don't want to. I wish I didn't have to. I'm pretty sure the guy's a creep."

I don't realize I'm tearing little shreds off the wrapper until the thing is confetti in my lap. I look back up at William, but of course he hasn't moved. "This is going to sound crazy, but I liked what you said the other night. I liked it way too much."

I sigh.

"I've never had that. I've never had anyone want to look after me that way. I've never had anyone so sure they'd want to stick around that long."

I bring my knees to my chest and hug them tight. What am I doing here talking to someone who can't answer. Especially when he told me to leave him alone?

"Thank you for not telling Sethos I'm not dancing for you anymore." Last night's payment appeared in my account today even though I didn't dance. "I wish I was, though."

I linger much longer than I should. I put my chin on my knees and just sit for a while in the silence. It doesn't feel so uncomfortable when you know there's no expectations. As the sun gets low on the horizon, I get up and stretch my legs. I'm still not ready to leave, but I know if I wait much longer the sun will go down and William will be mad. Before heading for the door, I lift up on my toes and press a kiss to his cold, hard cheek. "Thanks for listening."

Then I trudge down the stairs and back to the hostel for another dinner of cut-price dry sushi and an evening spent staring at the bottom of Melinda's bunk.

FOURTEEN

William

As soon as the sun dips below the horizon, I force my feet from my perch. With the memory of Jessie's sweet lips on my cheek, I stalk straight to the edge of the roof and leap off.

It doesn't take me long to find my way back to the inn where she's staying. Even if I couldn't follow her scent, the directions are etched into my mind from taking her home the other night.

It does me no good, though. I stalk backward and forward outside the building for hours, but Jessie makes no appearance. All I can do is replay what she said over and over until I'm gnashing my teeth, internally screaming in frustration.

She came to me for help. All I could do was sit there like a lump of rock while she poured out her fears and tried to talk to me. This is exactly why she doesn't need to be saddled with a man like me. A *monster* like me. Unfortunately, it doesn't stop me from needing to make everything right in her world.

I've never felt this way about anyone before. When I was human I was a selfish bastard. That's the reason I was cursed in the first place isn't it? But something about knowing she's mine—that she would be mine—makes me long to give her something. I can't provide for her, but I can protect her. That's one thing I can do. But I need to talk to her first. I'm not barging into this human inn and storming through the place searching for her and scaring all the other humans half to death. I'll only get her in trouble.

So I wait. Only she doesn't come.

When the sky turns yellow-gray, my movements grow jerky and my feet turn automatically for the theater. I try to resist. Try to buy a few more minutes as if that will make any difference. It's useless, though. Too soon the sky is growing light and my feet are fixed on my stone pedestal once more. I can feel another crack spreading over my cheek. Pressure from the constant grinding of my teeth marring my already misshapen body.

The next night I wake up angry. I tear open the door to the theater and storm through the building shouting for Sethos. "Where are you, you bastard? Show yourself! I know you can hear me, you fucking coward. I need to talk with you."

Sirens wail and lights flicker on as I move from room to room. I fling furniture about. I smash glasses and bottles of alcohol behind the bar. All of a sudden the hellish wails cut off and I smile. That can only mean one thing.

"Well, what is it?"

I turn and Sethos is standing behind me, leaning against a column in the foyer, his leonine tail flicking gently against his leg. "I thought my theater was burning down and I turn up and find it's just my guard having a tantrum. I'm not impressed du Buisson."

I don't give a flying fuck what impresses Sethos or not. I scowl at him. "How do I find Jessie?"

He lifts a brow. "You wait half a minute and she'll arrive for her final performance. That seems like the most logical answer. Though apparently I'm paying her for nothing, since here you are."

"You'll pay her for tonight if you want me to guard your damn theater."

"If this is what your protection looks like, I think I'll do without."

"Just tell me where she is, you asshole."

"You gave me your word." Sethos lifts his hand to inspect his sharp claws, ignoring my demand. "Your threats don't worry me."

I growl. "I said I'd guard it as long as I perched here each day, but I swear to heaven I'll uproot that fucking pedestal and move it myself if you don't tell me where to find her."

Sethos glares at me. Finally he sighs. "Did you claim her or not?"

My fists ball at my side. "None of your fucking business."

He rolls his eyes. "Clearly you didn't, or you wouldn't be this wound up. All I know is I hired her through Monstrous Deals. I can show you where to find the office. That's about it. They don't give out employee's addresses for obvious reasons."

"But she works for them? They'll know where she's working?"

"They might, if she's on a job for them." Sethos shrugs.

"Tell me where to find them."

Fifteen minutes later, I'm striding through the door of the Monster Bar, looking around the room, breathing in deep and hoping my Jessie is here. No luck. A tall, lanky werewolf behind the bar gives me a curious look. So I stalk over. "I need to find Jessie."

He gives me a sharp-toothed smile and a shrug. "Can't help you, brother. I can serve you a drink and show you how to request a booking through the app—"

"Fuck your app. Fuck your booking. She's not safe. I need to make sure she's safe."

The werewolf sets down the glass he's been polishing. He tilts his head and his nostrils flare. "What makes you say that, brother?"

He's listening, at least. His body language might look relaxed, but I can spot the predatory watchfulness in the set of his shoulders. I take a deep breath in and force myself to slow down. He might actually be able to help me, but I can't judge whether or not he might prove to be an ally yet. "She told me she was taking a job she wasn't sure about. She had a bad feeling about it."

His bushy brows lower. "Then why didn't you go with her?"

At my sides, my hands clench into fists. "It was daytime. There was nothing I could do. She left before I woke."

"And the job...?"

"Was this weekend. That's all I know."

Fishing a phone from his back pocket, the werewolf makes a call. Someone on the other end answers, but there's too much noise in the room for me to make out what is said.

"Got a client here who claims Jessie is in danger. Did she go out on a job for us tonight?"

After a pause, the guy's frown deepens. "OK. Will do."

He puts the phone back in his pocket and steps forward close to the bar. "She's not on an MD job tonight. Can you tell us anything else?"

I let out a huff of frustration. "Never mind. I'll deal with this myself."

Before I can turn to go, he leaps across the bar in a motion quicker than I anticipate and lays his hand on my arm. It takes everything I have not to break his arm, but that would only slow me down when he or someone else retaliates. "Hey! We look after our workers at Monstrous Deals. But if you want to help her, you have to give me something to go on."

I sigh. He's right. I wrack my brain for a moment. "I think she actually said it was a human job. I can't be sure. I guess I hoped I was wrong."

Bartender guy rubs at the scruffy beard which covers his chin. "OK. Anything else? Was it in a club? A private job?"

I think for a minute. If it was in a club, she'd have security. "It must be a private job." My tail swats the air. "This is taking too long. Her scent will be going cold."

Werewolf only snorts. "Scent? What scent? You don't even have a trail, or you'd be following it by now."

This is infuriating! I grip the edge of the bar and the wood creaks as I squeeze.

"Listen. If you give me a minute, I know a guy who knows a guy. I'll make some calls. We can trace the most likely venues and go from there."

I scowl. But I don't have any better options. "Fine."

A few minutes later, I'm pacing in front of the bar and the bartender turns to me with a grin. "I've got the names of five places that I think are our most likely options in the area. Which one do you want to try first?"

FIFTEEN

Jessie

I knew it.

I knew this job was a bad idea. Asshole hasn't even hired security. When I turned up, he told me his friend owns the bar and he's got the whole place tonight. Apparently, he's not short on friends either. His drunken mates fill the bar, cat-calling, and leering as soon as me and the other girl from Glitterbabes show up. Sandra, the other girl, is nervous as hell.

I don't blame her.

If we show fear now, though, the leering will turn into insults and grabbing. I know from experience. So I sway my hips and stride through the room to the open space set up at the back like the queen I am, ignoring the way it feels like every second guy I walk past is breathing down my neck. Sandra scurries along behind me and sticks closer than my shadow while I find the sound system and set up the music. "You wanna go first, babe?" I ask her.

She almost chokes on her own spit and shakes her head.

"You have stripped before, right?"

Sandra nods. "Yeah. But like only at this one club. I've never done a private show before. I thought it'd be different."

I give her a confident smile I don't feel. "Hey, don't worry. I've got you. Just act happy and watch what I do. If it starts to go south, we walk out, OK?"

"Yeah. Thanks."

The second the music starts and I begin to move, the heckling starts.

"Hey, scrawny, we paid to see ass. I hope you brought a friend."

"Yeah. She brought a friend. Bring her out."

"Oooh, yeah. I thought we were going to see a lesbian show."

I wrestle the smile back onto my face and keep going, swaying my hips and running my hands over my belly. This is far from the worst I've ever had. Their stupid lesbian comment shouldn't surprise me. So I do what I normally do when this sort of thing happens. I target the loudest heckler.

I figure he's probably doing it because somewhere deep down inside, he's missing something and he knows it. At least, that's what I tell myself. It helps if I kinda feel sorry for him. So I sashay over to the guy who made the dumb comment. He's handsome enough. His face is dominated by a thick retro-style mustache I hate, though. He has a deep cleft in his chin. Like an ass.

Running my hands over my body and lifting my breasts, I wink at Assface. "Think you could handle these scrawny thighs wrapped around your ears, huh?"

He smirks. "It'd be the best ride of your life, sweetheart."

I barely stop myself from laughing. There's no way anything beats the pussy licking William gave me the other night, especially not this asshole. I won't tell him that.

"Lay down on the floor, big guy. Let me give you a little personal attention."

He doesn't need to be told twice. He leaps out of his chair, hands his beer to his buddy and hurriedly takes his place in the center of the floor. His mates all cheer him on. Pretty soon, he's laying there and I've got him right where I want him. Feels good to stride over to him in my sky-high heels. I have nothing on but panties by this point, but I still feel powerful. And he's laying there thinking he's king shit. Win-win. I step my feet wide so I'm standing right above his face. The crowd whistles. Then I squat into a dance move and put my pussy right in his face, but only for a second. I snap back up and keep dancing, but my heart is beating fast. It's always risky dancing like this for someone volatile. I've got the situation under control, though.

Or so I think.

The next time I hover over him on my hands and knees, he grabs my ass. I struggle, but I'm not strong or quick enough to pull away in time. A warm, wet sensation over my cunt quickly turns cold and slimy. Assface just spat on my pussy. Fucking spat!

I scramble to my feet too shocked to keep dancing. "What the actual—"

That's all I get the chance to say. Next thing I know, a gray wall of muscle explodes through the crowd. William lifts my asshole customer from the floor by his collar. Holding him suspended in the air, William lets out a roar even I find a little bit terrifying. His wings extend. Guys to the left and right of me fall over themselves to get out of his way.

"Nobody spits on my princess. Nobody!"

Guys are shouting. Somewhere Sandra is screaming and I spare half a second to hope she's OK.

"Hey, hey. I didn't mean anything.." The guy is still dangling from William's grasp, stammering stupidly.

"You're right. You mean nothing. Less than nothing. And you're going to walk out of here without even looking at her again. You got that?"

He struggles. Perhaps he's trying to nod. "Y-yeah. Got it."

William drops him to the floor. and Assface crawls to his feet and rushes out of the bar. William takes a step closer to me, folding me into a wing as he glares around at the rest of the crowd who've gone awfully quiet. "And I'll give the rest of you miserable bastards five seconds to get the fuck out of here too, while you can still walk."

"Hey, you can't—"

"Five fucking seconds and counting!"

William's roar cuts off whatever the tall guy with the pot belly was about to say. His face goes very red and then very white. Then the whole lot of them are scrambling for the exits, snatching up jackets and keys and wallets. Chairs go flying. The door slams and we're alone.

I look up into the fiercest expression I think I've ever seen. His jaw is rigid. The dark scars across his cheek stand out in stark relief against the gray of his skin. His eyes burn with fury.

I shift uncomfortably, trying not to let my thighs touch. The cold wet patch staining my pussy feels a hundred times worse now it's just the two of us.

Then, just like that, William's stony face softens and he gathers me against his chest, petting my hair. "Sorry, princess."

His hand smooths over my hair in a motion so hypnotizing I almost can't reply. "W-what are you sorry for?"

"For not getting here sooner. For telling you to keep away. That was stupid."

Suddenly, I'm shaking. I grip his arm tight and press my lips together to hold back the tears I don't want to shed. Not for those assholes.

"So sorry, Jessie."

I shake my head against his chest. "You don't need to be sorry. I'm just glad you came. How did you find me?" I can't remember telling him the venue for this job. I'm surprised he even remembers much from the day I visited him, since he was sleeping while I talked.

Before William can answer, the door to the bar opens. I tense, expecting angry customers returning, or perhaps the owner here to chew us out about the damages. Then I recognize the bartender from the Monster Bar.

William glances around. The tall blond gives us a wave. "Cleared the rest of them off and phoned police to report an assault. They'll be here soon." He tips his head to indicate the broken furniture. "Though we should probably make ourselves scarce before that happens."

"I'll take you back to the inn." William's voice is a low rumble.

My immediate reaction is to cling to him. I'm not ready to leave the comforting circle of his arms and wings. Though I'm in desperate need of a shower. "No! Can I stay with you?"

William sighs. "There's nowhere I can take you that will be comfortable for you. Princess like you doesn't belong in a stone tower."

Maurice saunters over. "I have an apartment right near the Grand Theater. Spare room's yours, if you want it. Both of you. Come on."

I don't know what I did to deserve this incredibly chivalrous rescue, but I scoop up my clothes and dress quickly, not willing to look a gift horse in the mouth. I've had a good feeling all along about monsters over humans. Seems like I should have trusted my gut.

SIXTEEN

William

Jessie is still shaking when Maurice unlocks the door of his fifth floor apartment and shows us into the small living room. The apartment is off the ground, which is enough to make me feel better, and since it's decorated with mismatched furniture, I don't feel quite so awkward, worrying about how I'll fit my large frame and my wings and tail into the space without knocking something over. Reluctantly, I set Jessie down on her feet, but I keep my hand on her shoulder. If I'm not touching her right now, I'll lose it.

She glances back at me with a sad sort of half smile that feels like taking the butt of a lance in the guts. Then she turns back to the werewolf.

"Thank you for letting us come back here. And for coming to help me. I can't believe—" Her sentence is cut off when her voice wavers and I have to concentrate hard on not digging my claws into her when my hand tightens on her shoulder. I just want to pull her back into my arms and hold her, and tell her I'm sorry a hundred more times. But I'm sure she won't appreciate it. I'm lucky she's tolerating my presence, and I'm not trying to do anything to jeopardize that.

Maurice waves away her thanks. "Che nada. Listen, I have to go back to work in a mo', but you're welcome to stay. Stay the night. Stay longer. Whatever you need."

"Oh no. I'd just love to have a shower, really. And I'll get out of your hair once I've had a chance to talk with William."

Inside the stone cage of my chest, my heart flutters wildly, wondering what she wants to say. Probably, 'leave me the fuck alone, you creep'. I sigh. I'm not sure I'll be able to, even if she asked me.

Maurice goes to a cupboard in the hallway and takes out two large towels, one blue and one green. It seems nothing in his home matches and I like him more for it. He's my type of bloke. Not pretentious. You can tell he wears his heart on his sleeve. "Here. Bathroom's the second door on the right. And the first door is the spare room. I mean it. You make yourselves at home. Anything I can grab you before I go?"

Jessie shakes her head. I'd love to ask him to get her something to eat, but I sense that would only make her more uncomfortable, so I resist. I don't love how much I owe this guy, but I figure a meal is nothing compared to the debt I have to repay him. I'll find a way to work it off.

A few minutes later, the front door clicks shut and we're alone. Jessie fidgets with the button on her jacket. "I'll just take that shower, OK?"

"Course." I nod and wish something I could say would ease the tension I feel in her tight muscles and her trembling lip.

She starts undressing, not stopping at the jacket, which she hands to me. As she slips her black dress over her head, I swallow thickly and turn away.

A tsk from behind me makes me turn. "What are you doing, you big dork? You've already seen everything."

I shrug. "Now feels different. You're not putting on a show."

She gives me a little smile. "No, but I don't mind."

Unable to speak, I shake my head and turn away again. This feels important. I'm determined to treat my beautiful girl like the treasure she is.

A few moments later, I hear the patter of water in the bathroom and dig my claws into my palms to hold firm to my resolve. It doesn't stop me picturing the way the hot water would sluice down her perfect curves, washing over the smooth skin I long to caress. I palm down my swelling cock beneath my loincloth and jump when Jessie calls to me from the bathroom. "Oh crap. Hey, William, will you look and see if you can find some soap for me?"

I squeeze my eyes closed and pray for strength before I enter the steamy room and hunt around in the drawers of the cabinet doing my best not to notice the naked flesh I see from the corner of my eye through the misted glass. But that's all it takes to have me semi-hard and dreaming of more. I find a small white square of soap and open the shower door, thrusting my hand inside while averting my eyes.

"Thanks."

When I step out of the bathroom, I slump back against the door, ignoring the way it presses my wings against my back. The devil, if he really exists, surely knows he owns my miserable soul already. It's beyond me why he still needs to send such temptation to me as if there's any chance I could redeem myself.

The door opens and I jump aside. Thank heavens, when she steps out of the bathroom, she has one towel wrapped around her hair like a turban and one wrapped around her luscious body. She wrinkles her nose. "I still feel dirty. I don't know if I'll ever feel clean again."

My tipping point is when her wry smile flips into a frown and a tear trickles down her cheek. I gather her into my arms and press a kiss to the towel. "Princess, you are perfect. No matter what anyone does. Some gems are too bright to tarnish."

It near wrenches my heart from my ribcage when I feel her tremble and hear her quiet sniff. "Hold me for a while?"

As if I have any choice. I'd do anything she asked. Well, anything except leave her, let her go. That I can't do. I was a fool to think I could push her away and somehow forget her. There's no question in my mind now that she's mine. Or rather, I'm hers. I'm bound to her as surely as if I've taken a vow of service. I'll love her until my body turns to dust.

I lead her gently to the room Maurice said was the spare room and we lay on the bed. It's too small for me. My wings and tail and legs hang over the edge. But I tuck myself into the smallest shape I can manage and cradle her in my arms, thankful for the chance to be what she needs.

After a while, she snuggles closer and sighs. "We should probably talk."

I repress a groan. Here is the part where she tells me to keep away from her and I have to let her down. To my surprise, she tips her chin to look up at me and gives me a shy smile. "I don't suppose you'd be prepared to revisit the whole stay away thing?"

I flounder with my answer and she looks down, her lashes shielding her eyes, but not the hurt. Using my finger, I gently lift her chin until she's looking at me again. "You know it doesn't have anything to do with you, angel? You know that, don't you?"

The lance twists in my gut when the sparkle of moisture beneath her lashes tells me she doesn't. "Princess, it's me. I don't know how to make you believe. Well, I do, but I don't want to do it..."

She looks up at me and I sigh.

"Listen. If me being a monster isn't enough to put you off, I should tell you what I did to get myself in this state."

"OK." She just looks at me as if what I'm about to say won't send her running.

Running a hand over my hair, I try to gather the words. "I'm a thief. That's what it boils down to. I was traveling a long way from home. The trip had cost me more than I anticipated and I was running low on funds. Originally, I traveled with a large group. An army, I suppose. Eventually a few of us broke away from the main group and we came across a family. They were traveling in the same direction we were. They begged us to protect them. So we said we would. They said they didn't have much to give, but they promised to share what they had with us and they shared their food. But, when one of the other knights I was with found their stash of jewelry, he accused them of lying. It was late in the night. They pleaded with us to leave them their treasure. It was all they had. I fought the others and promised to protect them."

I can't look at her when I tell the next part.

"But while they were sleeping the next night, I took their treasure and left them there. I didn't get far." I spread my arms wide to remind her of my monstrous form. "Turns out there was a curse laid on the treasure. I tried to go back the night I found out I was cursed. But when I found them, someone else had got there first. It wasn't pretty. I'd left them with no protection and no money. So I was never able to return the treasure. And here I am."

I wince, imagining a look of disdain on her pretty features in the silence. But when I look, her expression is harder to read than that.

"Do you regret it?"

I nod. "With every fiber of my being. I've had many years to think about how wrong it was to take advantage of the vulnerable like that."

She nods. "We all make mistakes. I guess most of us are lucky those mistakes don't stain us forever." There's a pause and it feels heavy. "I hope mine don't. I hope I'm not just that filthy slut to assholes like that forever."

I shake my head again, reaching for her. "What you do with your body is not a mistake. It's your choice. It was a mistake of those bastards to think they had any right to what doesn't belong to them."

She smiles. "Well you certainly came to my rescue when I needed it. Protected me and asked nothing in return."

Her words lighten my heart just a little. Perhaps she's right. Perhaps I have improved.

She moves closer still and my heart practically floats out of my chest. I stop her when she leans in to kiss me. "Jessie, are you sure? Because I promise you, there's nothing I want more. Nothing would make me happier than to be near you."

Her frown turns into a grin. "Really?"

I nod. "Really."

Her grin turns wicked and her hand slides down my belly. "Nothing?"

Christ alive, a man can only take so much temptation! My cock springs to life and I groan when her fingertips trace lower. I make myself put my hand on hers and stop her.

"But you don't have to do that. You don't have to do anything you don't want to do."

She tugs her hand from beneath mine and I let her. Then she takes me off guard by reaching up to pull on my horn and bring our foreheads together. "William, what I want is to feel your hands and mouth and skin on mine. I want you to make me feel like you did the other night. Because I don't want to end this day feeling like the slut someone spat on. I want to end it feeling like your princess."

God in His heaven, how can I resist?

SEVENTEEN

GIVEN TO THE GARGOYLE

Jessie

William's eyes widen and I have a moment to process the fact that he really didn't expect anything from me tonight. Nothing at all. Not even after he walked in on my stripping for those assholes. Not even after witnessing my humiliation. Instead of walking away in disgust, he's treating me like some treasure. Not even after he had to come to my rescue like a freaking hero from a storybook.

His words about my being a gem that can't be tarnished are still resounding in my heart when he rolls me onto my back and the delicious weight of his large body nestles between my thighs. "Ah, Jessie, you are the most beautiful creature I've ever seen."

He lifts my hands above my head, but doesn't keep me pinned there, though he easily could. Instead, he runs rough palms down my arms. When he finally reaches my breasts, I'm aching for his touch there. He cups them tenderly. "The most perfect treasure."

My back is arching off the bed when he finally lowers his lips to my skin. His hot mouth envelops half my breast as he suckles first one, then the other. He pushes my breasts together to feast on them as if he could stay and do nothing else for the rest of the night.

Eventually, he raises his head. When he does, we're both breathing unevenly.

"You know what I'm going to ask you, don't you?"

I nod. "I am. I'm sure. I want this."

"And you know that this makes me yours? I won't say it makes you mine. In my heart it's true already, but the only person who can make that choice is you. Once I get inside that

107

glorious little pussy, that's it. I'm done for. You'll never be rid of me."

I reach down and stroke his cheek. He stills, leaning into my light touch.

"I don't want to be rid of you, you dork. That's what I'm trying to say. I want that. I want you. And if you're mine, then I'm yours. If you'll have me."

A smile plays at the edge of his lips, but he grows serious again quickly. "And there's the ah... the knot."

I tip my head to the side. "The knot?"

Is that color deepening across his cheeks? Above us, his wings flick open and closed. "My knot. At the base of my cock. It expands when I come."

I raise my brows. "You get bigger?" I glance down, already aware of just how big he feels.

He swallows. "I... yes." William hangs his head and I touch his face to lift his gaze to mine again.

I can only chuckle. Most guys would be boasting. Not my sweet gargoyle. "Believe me, it's not a problem. As long as you want me."

Turning his head, he presses a kiss to the center of my palm, then another to my wrist. His mouth trails up my arm until his lips hover above mine. "Of course I want you, Jessie. I want no one else but you."

William cups the back of my neck and lowers his mouth to mine. Soon my worries are forgotten in a kiss so passionate I almost forget to breathe. His lips should feel rough and hard. They still look as if they're chiseled from stone. But his kiss is tender, soft. Loving. I've never been kissed like this.

GIVEN TO THE GARGOYLE

Neither of us last long only kissing, though. Soon I can't resist sliding my hands over his broad shoulders. I wrap my legs around his hips and squeeze him tight.

William groans. His hips rock, thrusting a bulging cock against my inner thigh, moving in a rhythm that makes me ache with want.

I want to be filled by this gentle giant. I want to be possessed by this man who looks at me as if there's nothing else grounding him to Earth. And, of course, I very much want to feel how that thick hard cock moves inside me.

My towel is long gone. The one binding my hair has come free and my damp locks spill out over the pillow. William's large hand slides over my belly and teases the hair at my mound and I gasp.

He growls, the sound reverberating through my body, centering on my clit in delicious waves of sensation. "Spread those cunny lips for me, gorgeous. Let me see all of you."

I part my legs wide as he shifts from the bed to the floor. Then he tugs me forward until my ass rests at the edge of the bed right under his hungry mouth. I moan while he devours that part of me. He laves my pussy with long strokes of his tongue. He plants his lips over my clit and draws pleasure from me that bows my back and has me clutching his horns. "William!"

Calling his name only makes him more ferocious in his enthusiasm. His hands reach beneath me, cupping my ass and gathering me closer. His hungry noises against my wet and swollen flesh are almost enough to tip me over the edge.

When he flicks my clit with the tip of his tongue, I finally do. My orgasm tears through me with an intensity matching his fervor. I cling to him, riding wave after wave, until I'm spent and the climax fades to lingering sweetness.

By the time he lifts his head, I'm laughing softly.

"Was that good, princess?"

"So good. So, so good."

"Will I keep going?"

I shake my head. "Fuck me? I want to feel you inside me."

His claws tighten at my hips. "Oh, Jessie. Sweet, angel. I want nothing more."

Pulling him over me, I reach between us and help guide him to me. I'm wet and tender from his mouth. Just the tip of his heated erection pressing against me is ecstasy. We moan together when he rocks his hips and presses deeper still. The stretch of being filled is intense and not enough all at once.

When he pauses, I tell him, "Keep going."

He's braced on strong arms, hovering above me. I can see the strain in his tense muscles and the veins standing out beneath marbled gray skin. "I don't want to hurt you."

I smile and use my heels at his butt to encourage him. "Oh, honey, you won't."

He thrusts again, but he's still only barely penetrating me. He's so far from giving me everything. "William, please!"

He shakes his head. Then he rolls us again and I grin when he pulls me on top. "You do it, princess. That way I know you're taking only as much as you want."

"Mmm." I'm practically purring as I push down over him. "God, you feel amazing."

William lets out a soft curse as I breathe out and take him deeper. Then I roll my hips and feel the friction of my clit against his pelvic bone and know I have him all the way.

"Sweet mother of god, you are so tight, woman."

I laugh and lift up, coming back down slowly, loving the way his lips part and his mouth hangs open as I work his cock in and out of me. "Guess it was worth all those kegels, huh?"

William grunts. His hips lift to meet mine on the next roll of my body. "I don't know what the fuck a kegels is, but I would sell my soul if I could stay inside you for the rest of my days."

My giggle rapidly turns into a groan and then I'm too focused to speak, to laugh. All I can do is move over his cock while his hands at my hips lift me up and down, speeding my rhythm until the slap, slap of our bodies rises to fill the room.

"Fuck, fuck!" William's curses increase with our speed.

I feel my own climax rising, gripping my core. My belly clenches. I dig my nails into William's upper arms.

He pulls me down against him and I grind on him as my body spasms and I'm coming. Only I'm coming around a cock that's swelling to fill me fuller until I can't move. I can't think. There's only the pleasure and his strong hands on me, and most of all his cock inside me. I sink down onto his chest, pressing my face to the sweaty, masculine-smelling warmth. I let myself float in the feeling he might actually never let me go.

The last thing I remember before I drift is the sound of his heartbeat in my ear. The pounding slows to a gentle rhythm and lulls me to sleep. How strange I thought he was only a statue when I first saw him. I don't think another person in my life has treated me with so much warmth and tenderness ever before. It's not that people are unkind. I'm overwhelmed by the kind things Maurice has done and the things Rachel said to me only a few days ago. It's just, this creature who looks like he's made of stone actually has the softest heart I've ever known.

EIGHTEEN

GIVEN TO THE GARGOYLE

William

My knot is softening. I don't move at first, too content cradling Jessie on my chest and listening to her soft sighs while I trace her flawless skin with the backs of my claws. Then a flood of moisture has me reaching for one of her discarded towels, so Maurice doesn't have to clean up after us. I don't need another reason to owe the guy.

Jessie stirs and lifts her head to look up at me. "God, that was good."

Her smile is so dazzling my cock is in danger of growing hard again. I can't help the answering smile that lifts the corner of my mouth. "Yeah?"

"Mmm. Yeah. You're amazing."

Using my hands on her ass to grind her against me I let her feel my growing length inside her. "Keep talking like that, princess and we'll be right back at the beginning again."

Christ! She licks her lips and her pussy clenches around me like she did it on purpose. She fucking did. I groan when she does it again.

"Would that be so bad?"

I'm helpless under her as she rocks her hips and pleasure tightens my belly. "Oh fuck. I don't know. You tell me." I would have thought she'd be sore after taking my cock. I'm not small and the knot as well...

Jessie plants her hands on the middle of my chest and grins. "I'm not ready to let you go yet. So why don't you show me what you got?"

I growl and flip her to her back, suddenly feeling a hell of a lot better about just how well she can take me. She just beams up at me, then tugs me down by the horns for a kiss.

It's hard to reach while I'm still inside her. I'm so much larger, but I manage it. The taste of her lips is sweet and rich and mingles with the flavor of her cunny, which lingers on my lips and chin. I'd love to drink my fill of her again, but my princess is determined to have my cock in her, and the way her tight little pussy grips me makes me reluctant to be anywhere else. God she's wet. The sounds our bodies make as I plunge into her have me even harder. Her little cunny is full of me. Full of my cock, my come. She stretches perfectly to take me. Her legs wrap around my hips and draw me close and every part of her is soft and welcoming.

My head is spinning, my body humming with pleasure. My wings spread wide. Something on the nightstand crashes to the floor and I grunt out a curse. Jessie only laughs. "Harder."

Christ, this woman!

"Harder, babe. I want to feel you for days."

I pull out with a growl and flip her to her belly. I'm so lost in it I don't even wait. I pull her hips up, exposing her plump pink lips and her dripping pussy.

Jessie moans when I enter her again. Thank god, because I'm not gentle. I'm too far gone. Her pleas for me to fuck her harder tipped me over the edge.

She reaches between her legs to play with herself and I brush away her hand, replacing it with my own. "You need something princess, then you ask me. It's my pleasure to give it to you. You don't have to do anything, except let me make you feel more pleasure than you ever felt before."

She cries out when I rub her in time with my thrusts. With one hand, I clutch her hip, bringing her back against me while my hips thrust over and over. I work her little nub with my other hand until I find the pressure and rhythm that makes her buck. A few more hard circles of her bud and pounding thrusts of my cock, she screams my name.

"William!"

The sound is everything I never knew I needed.

Then I'm coming with her, my knot swelling again and my body trembling with my release. At the last moment, I twist to the side so I don't crush her. I pull her down so I can curl my larger body around hers and press a kiss to her hair, sighing with contentment. We lay together, me savoring the knot holding her here where I can breathe in her scent and stay surrounded by her, buried in her.

Eventually, she says, "William?"

"Hmm?" I can barely keep my eyes open, though it's still full dark.

"I wish you could stay with me."

"Not going anywhere, princess. Not until daylight."

"That's what I mean. I like having you near, even when you can't talk to me. It just makes me feel better."

I have to fight the instinct to crush her smaller body to mine. If I didn't have to, I'd never let her go. I sigh. "The curse—"

"I know." Jessie lifts my hand to her lips to give me a gentle kiss. "I know. Will you let me come visit you in the daytime, while you're sleeping? And at night, of course when I'm not working?"

"Of course. You won't be able to keep me away while I'm awake. Not now."

She makes a contented little sound and snuggles in, the movement wiggling her rounded ass against my groin, giving my cock ideas. You'd think he'd be spent, but apparently, he could be persuaded to perform again. I squash that thought, not wanting to leave Jessie sore.

"I'll still have to work." Her tone is cautious.

I kiss her hair. "I know. I don't like it, but I know. I should be able to provide for you now you're my mate. But I can't. You won't dance alone again, though. I'll come with you. At least, I can protect you."

"Aww. Don't you have to guard the theater? Isn't that what Sethos made you promise?"

I huff. "Sethos can burn in hell for all I care." I gave him my word, though. Now I wish I hadn't. Jessie interrupts my sullen thoughts.

"I wish I could work at the theater. Not stripping. I want to act. But I've never even got as far as audition for any production at the Grand."

I consider her words. "There haven't been any productions there for months. But now I'm awake and able to guard it properly, Sethos intends to reopen. I'll just remind him that he would be wise to keep me motivated to protect the place. And the thing that would motivate me most is if my princess is on center stage."

Jessie laughs. "I'd be happy with a role as someone's backup dancer or a non-speaking part. But if you think you can get me an audition, I won't complain."

I tuck my top wing over her as if I can gather her closer. "I'll make it happen, princess. You'll see."

Nothing but the best for my princess from now on. I just gotta find a way of keeping that promise before I speak it out loud.

GIVEN TO THE GARGOYLE

We lay like that until I feel the drag of the sun rising and know it's time to leave. All the while my mind works over the thing that's bothering me: how can I find or make enough money to take care of my mate? Even when I was human, I never had much. What I did have, I sold to buy supplies on my ill-fated journey. Sold what didn't belong to me as well, which is what got me into this stone prison in the first place. What have I got to show for it now? A bag of coins of no use to anyone. The value of the silver is nothing in today's world. The coins can no longer be used. I'm as useless to my mate as they are.

NINETEEN

GIVEN TO THE GARGOYLE

Jessie

I stare at my reflection in the illuminated mirror. I hardly recognize myself behind the heavy stage makeup and the blonde wig. This is it. I'm really here. I'm about to step out onto center stage of the Grand Theater and perform in my very first show. It's not the lead role. I don't care, though. I've never been so close to everything I want.

Everyone else has already left the communal dressing room. They'll be waiting backstage. Opening the door to the corridor a crack, I spot William pacing. "Psst."

He looks over immediately, wings lifting and tucking tight against his back again in agitation. I think he's more nervous than I am.

"Come here!"

He strides to my door in two quick steps. "What is it? Is something wrong? Should I get Tara back again?"

I shake my head. "My makeup is fine. My costume is fine. Nothing's wrong. I just need a little kiss for luck."

Before he can reply, I wrap both my arms around one of his and tug him inside the dressing room, then close the door behind us. The slightly bemused look on his otherwise stoic features makes me smile every time I stretch up to kiss him. I love it so much I do it all the time. He always reacts the same way, as if he can't believe I'd want to. As if he hasn't realized by now how much I adore my big man mountain.

His kiss tonight is hesitant. After only a few moments, he pulls back, laying two gentle hands on my arms. "Don't let me ruin your makeup."

I laugh. "I think this stuff is going to need industrial strength cleaner to get it off. Don't worry. Besides, I'm not feeling nearly lucky enough yet." Ignoring his protests, I fling my arms around his neck so he's forced to catch me up. Then I wrap my legs around his hips. That's more like it.

"Jessie!"

He doesn't resist for long, though, when I press my lips to his and slick my tongue against his. With a groan, he slides his hands to my ass and hungrily returns my kiss. Somehow, I end up with my ass on the counter in front of the mirror, his lean hips cradled against me and a growing bulge against my sex evidence his enthusiasm matches mine, despite his worries.

"If we're quick we have time," I murmur against his mouth when he lets me up for air.

He curses. "Christ, Jessie. I don't think that's a good idea. My knot—"

I roll my hips, loving the way his thick length grazes against my pussy. An answering sizzle of pleasure sparks low in my belly. "Mmm, I love your knot."

His laughter is tortured. I press kisses all along his chiseled jaw when he tries to escape me. "You need to get out there. And so should I. I should be scanning for threats."

"Pffft. What threats? Sethos is crazy. Who would burn down a theater? Honestly, people are way more relaxed about monsters these days. There's nothing to worry about."

Most of the cast are supes of one kind or another. Not that it bothers me. I love it. But I guess some human actors weren't so keen. When Sethos announced the show, he didn't get much interest outside the monster community. So we're a mishmash of human and monster actors, professional and semi-professional. We're good, though. Even if I say so myself. I just know this show is going to blow away the critics.

William places a final kiss on my forehead and carefully sets me on my feet. When I reach for him again, his hand on my shoulder is enough to prevent me. "I need to let this calm down." He gestures at the enormous bulge beneath his loincloth, which of course draws my gaze.

I bite my lip and he lets out another ragged curse. "Jessie, please!"

"OK, OK. But promise me you'll come right back here after the show. I don't wanna wait until we get back home."

Maurice will probably still be out, but I can't help feeling a little guilty at how much noise we make. Luckily, my new housemate works nights, so we often have the place to ourselves, but I know it makes William uncomfortable. At least, I think that's what makes him walk around like he's got the weight of the world on his broad shoulders. He's been doing everything he can to repay the favor he thinks he owes Maurice, ever since the night the two of them rescued me. Although, my sweet new friend has told William repeatedly that's unnecessary.

William gives me a sheepish smile. "You're mad if you think I could stay away longer than that. But I really should go now and make sure everything is safe."

Reluctantly, I let him go and turn to check my costume a final time. On the table in front of me, my phone screen lights up and I glance down to see I have a new follower. One of many this week as we stepped up promo for the show. Dismissing the notification, I tuck my phone into my handbag. Then I begin my vocal warm-ups. Time to knock 'em dead!

The final note of my solo hangs in the air of the packed theater for three long seconds. Then the room erupts into applause and cheers and I'm clenching my jaw to hold the mournful expression for the end of the scene, rather than letting my smile spread across my face. I did it. They love it.

I bask a moment more before breaking the spell and getting to my feet. Turning from the audience toward the other actors on stage, I cue the applause to stop.

The moment is only topped when we all run out onto stage front for the final curtain call. Beyond the bright lights of the theater, I spot a few people at the front getting to their feet. More and more rise until almost the whole audience is standing, cheering, and whistling. A genuine standing ovation. I grip the hands of the actors to my right and left tighter as we take a final bow.

Backstage, we're full of nervous energy. With hugs and tears and so many voices talking and laughing at once, it's hard to keep track. I'm excited too. Of course I am.

Brittney, the other actor in the heartbreak scene with me, pulls me into a huge squealing hug. "Oh my god, Jessie! That high note. I thought I was going to cry. You just nailed it tonight."

I lean back to grin at her. "Really? Thank you! Your dance was just beautiful. Flawless."

She blushes and tucks her hair behind one ear. "I'm not as good as you, though. Hey, a few of us are going out for drinks later. You wanna come?"

My eyes dart toward the door. William will be waiting for me somewhere quiet. I've told him before not to be shy about anyone knowing we're together, but he always hangs back when I'm with the cast. "Let me go find William and see what he's doing."

Brittney nods. "Sure. I hope I see you later."

When I look out into the corridor, it's empty except for a box of wigs and some spare lights waiting to be put into storage. He's not inside the dressing room either. Not even waiting outside. I pull off my wig and change out of my costume, quickly wiping away most of the makeup. When I'm back in my leggings and oversize sweater, I grab my handbag and head for the east tower. Glancing down at my phone, I frown when a new message request pops up. It's a user I don't recognize. I open it anyway, figuring it's probably someone who saw the show and wants to say something nice. I mean, I hope it's something nice!

The message that pops up on my screen makes me stumble up the last step.

PhatOne: You can dress up like a virgin, but I know what a little slut you are. I'll always know.

I block the profile and delete the message, shoving my phone back in my handbag with a shaking hand. Thankfully, I forget all about that asshole when I open the door to the tower and see William sitting on the edge of the archway with his head in his hands.

"Hey you!"

He turns and gives me a sad smile as I approach. "Hey, you."

He lets me pull his head against my chest in a hug. Then he looks up at me and shakes his head. "You're amazing, you know that?"

"What are you doing sitting up here all alone?"

William sighs. "Protecting the theater. Protecting you."

I sit, tucking myself against his side and he puts a wing around me to keep me warm. "You know you can do that better when you're with me."

He shakes his head. "I don't want to get in the way."

"You're not in the way." I try to nudge him with my shoulder, but he's basically a giant boulder, so I only overbalance myself. William's arm keeps me from tipping over the other way. "Hey, some of the cast are going for drinks in a little while. Wanna come? I want to introduce you to everyone."

William gives me a long look. "You don't want that."

"Why not?"

"I'm not good with people. I got too used to being on my own."

"You're good with me. And Maurice."

He snorts. "Two of the easiest people to get along with ever. That doesn't count."

"It counts. You don't even have to say anything. I just like having you around."

He shakes his head again sadly. "I have to stay here. I gave Sethos my word."

I pout. "God, he's a drama queen. No one is going to burn down the theater. Should I stay here with you?"

"No, princess. You go have a good time. Come back and visit me before morning?"

I press a kiss to his nose as I rise to my feet. "Of course. I won't be long. Just a couple of drinks. I can sleep late tomorrow 'cause I don't have to be here until five."

His deep voice rumbles a goodbye. I turn and give him a final wave before I leave the tower. I really wish he wasn't bound to his word or so reserved in front of others. I wish he could see what I see when I look at him. What I see is the most perfect guy I've ever known. I just wish I could get it through his thick skull.

TWENTY

GIVEN TO THE GARGOYLE

William

I hate when she's far from me. Well, far is a relative term really. I hate when she's out of arm's reach. But I can't hold her back from celebrating her success.

She was absolutely magnificent on stage. Naturally I watched the whole performance from my rooftop tower. Jessie was beautiful, of course. Even beneath the heavy makeup that partially disguises her natural beauty, she is stunning. Tonight I could have closed my eyes and flown on the notes of her song. I've heard it many times each day since she first began rehearsing the part. Every single time, the achingly sweet melody is a current of wind beneath the wings of my soul.

Of course, I kept my eyes open. I didn't want to miss a moment. I also didn't want to miss any potential threat. I alternated watching my princess with scanning the outside of the theater and watching the crowd. The ones I could see anyway. I'm relieved now the theater is emptying and contented audience members are walking out onto the winter streets. Jessie walks out with a group of other cast members. She's wearing a thick warm jacket against the cold that doesn't touch my skin anymore. Turning, she blows a kiss up toward me before the group heads down a narrow side street and out of view.

After about an hour, I relax. Seems like Sethos might have been worrying about nothing. He seemed to think opening night held the highest risk. So, I guess I can worry a little less tomorrow and the night after that and the night after that. I sigh, thinking how many nights it might take for me to trust nothing bad will happen to my angel.

Shaking out stiff limbs, I climb down from my perch and turn to lift the heavy marble, revealing the small hole beneath. I bend and lift out the pouch, carefully supporting the worn leather in my large hands to keep it from tearing.

The coins inside spill out into my palm when I tip the bag. I shake my head. I don't even know why I've taken them out again. Not like counting them will produce any more. It's a bitter irony that this treasure is just as much a curse on me now as it ever was. From the center of the pile, a single golden ring mockingly winks at me.

I wish I never set eyes on the damn things. Only then, I would never have been cursed at all, and I'd have lived out my natural life to die centuries ago, never having met the love of my life.

I shove the measly stash back into its bag and the bag back into my keeping place. Returning the stone perch to its usual position, I straighten to see Sethos watching me. I step instinctively over the marble plinth, though I don't think he saw me. Still, you can never trust a sphinx with your gold, and I'd trust Sethos even less than most. "What do you want?"

His fur-tipped tail flicks against his leg. "Just to make sure you're doing what you promised."

I spread my arms wide. "Here I am. I haven't left."

"Glad to see it." He prowls up the archway and leans casually against the stone. "It went well tonight. Very well."

I lift my shoulders in a shrug. Does he want to chat now as if we are friends? "Did it?"

He smirks at me. "That girl of yours is a rare find. I'm glad you suggested I audition her. I think I've had more comments about her solo than any other part of the production. I'll have to have her in the lead role next time."

I fold my arms across my chest with a grunt. Of course, Jessie is amazing. Of course, she should have the lead role. Only a small part of me tenses at the suggestion. How much more risk will there be when she's on every poster and at the forefront of people's minds. It's what she wants though, and I'm happy for her. I'll just have to work harder to keep her safe.

Eventually, he leaves me alone after he's berated me again about the promise I made to keep his precious theater safe. As if I'd let it burn down when it represents all my princess's dreams.

I gaze out into the dark night and wait for her to come back to me.

Her scent on the night breeze comes to me first. It's deep and rich and sweet as ever. I spot her walking alone down a dark street between two smaller buildings and my wings twitch in frustration. She should have gotten a ride or walked with a friend. I don't like her out late alone. I don't like that she doesn't have a way of contacting me. I would have come to get her if I had known.

A billboard advertising the show blocks my view of part of the street. As the real figure of Jessie slips behind her printed likeness, a shard of fear spikes my gut. Moments later, I realize why. Jessie's scent changes from sweet to acrid.

I need no further motivation. I spread my wings and spring from the tower, cursing when I land on top of the billboard and still can't spot her.

Then I glance down and see her running. She's moved faster than I anticipated. Swooping from above, I land on the street beside her and catch her when she screams and stumbles. "William! You scared me!"

Hastily, I search the darkness, but find no threat. "What happened?"

Jessie looks behind her, but shakes her head. "I just... I thought I heard something. Stupid, right?" She's breathing hard. Harder than the short run alone should warrant.

I growl. "Not stupid. Why were you walking alone? *That* was stupid."

She swats my chest. "It wasn't far. Brittney walked me to the corner of Hart Row."

"Hmph." I don't want to argue, though. So I stoop and gather her into my arms, then spread wide my wings and launch us into the air. Jessie throws her arms around my neck and buries her face against my shoulder. When I alight on the roof of the theater and go to set her down, she clings to me.

"Hold me a little longer?" She's shivering and I suddenly realize it's not the cold, but fear.

"What happened?" My growl is rougher than I'd like, but she only snuggles closer.

"I just got some nasty messages. That's all. Then I thought there was someone following me, but when I looked around there was no one. It's stupid. Just a dumb fear in the dark. You're right. I should have taken the main street or taken a cab."

I brush a large, clumsy hand over her hair, marveling at how smooth and soft it is. Jessie sighs. "Just shitty words, right?"

I frown, hating that something I didn't see coming has her so shaken. "What words? What were the messages?"

She shrugs. "Just some asshole calling me names. Forget it, OK? I just want to forget it."

I hold her against me as tight as I dare. "OK, princess. Whatever you want. We'll forget it."

TWENTY
ONE

GIVEN TO THE GARGOYLE

Jessie

The room I rent from Maurice is only a few blocks away from the theater. William still insists on flying me there, though. I can make absolutely no complaints.

Despite my jacket, I'm a little cold by the time his clawed feet grip the iron rail of the tiny balcony outside the living room. He carefully sets me down and waits until I've unlocked the door and gone inside before he folds his wings and ducks under the doorframe to follow.

"Are you hungry?" he asks.

I shake my head. "I ate already. Come to bed." I give him a look he can't misinterpret and he lets out a long huff of breath.

"Careful, woman. You know what those words and that look does to me."

I grin. "I'm counting on it."

He strides forward and puts his hands on my hips, steering me backward around the furniture and into my room.

It's simple. I've got only a few odds and ends other than the basic bed and desk. It's still a squeeze for William's large frame to fit. As soon as the backs of my legs hit the mattress, I fall onto the bed, clinging to William and pulling him down with me. Of course, he uses his wings and his strong arms to keep most of his weight from crushing me, but I still love the feel of him on top of me and between my thighs.

A deep rumble from his chest shoots straight to my clit when I roll my hips and draw him into a kiss. I love the feel of his thick body pinning me in place and the scratchy texture of his face when he trails kisses along my jaw. Most of all, I love the way he breathes my name like a prayer when he pulls back and tugs down my leggings. revealing my lacy black thong. He traces the curves of my waist and hips with reverent hands and slips a claw beneath the elastic to draw them aside.

I gasp with pleasure and my body bucks when his thumb glides through my wetness to the exact place beneath my clit where I'm longing for his touch. When I can breathe again, I lift on my elbows to look down at him, to see the flecks of deep black in his gray eyes when he looks up at me from between my thighs.

"Sweet Christ, was there ever anything so beautiful?" His words are low and raspy. His thumb makes slow circles around my clit until I moan.

"God, I'd like to have a painting made of you just like this. Spread out for me like this. I'd like to hang it somewhere so I could look at you all day."

I laugh softly. "I'll take some pictures for you sometime."

"Mmm." William draws another layer of moisture from my opening through my sensitive folds and swirls it around my clit. "Perfection. Look how wet and juicy you are for me."

I nod. "Always."

"And is my princess ready to come for me now? Ready for me to make you feel good?"

"Yes."

William doesn't wait any longer. As soon as the word leaves my lips, he speeds up his motions. When the pleasure becomes too intense, I flop back onto the bed and fist the sheets in my hands while my belly tightens and my pussy clenches.

His slick finger slides backward and forward in a steady rhythm. When I get closer, I instinctively try to close my thighs. William chuckles. "No, princess. No escaping me."

Then he flips me over onto my belly and pins my hands behind my back with one firm hand.

He nudges my legs open wider with his knee. "Spread for me, princess. That's it."

I let out a keening cry when his thick fingers spear into me, curling against the walls of my pussy.

"Now come for me, and don't stop coming until I tell you."

I moan into the bedding as he fucks me with two fingers. I'm almost loud enough to drown out the wet sounds we make. The feeling only gets better when he lets go of my hands and gives my ass a resounding smack, making me clench around his invasion.

"Come, angel. Come for me."

My body obeys, quaking and shuddering, as he continues to thrust into me over and over.

"That's my good girl. Give it to me. Don't stop."

I keep coming around his fingers as the pleasure goes on and on. My legs give out and I'm held up only by his strength. My wetness floods his hand and runs down my thighs.

William gives a growl of satisfaction. One large hand squeezes my ass. "There you go, gorgeous. That's right. God, you're a good fucking girl."

My pussy gives a final clench at his sweet, possessive words. Then he withdraws his fingers, leaving me strangely empty. I only feel it for a moment, though. William lifts me and tucks me into bed, curls his large body around mine, and strokes my hair. Vaguely, I wonder if he wants to come, too, but his claws brushing through my hair feel too good. So I let go and drift on the sea of pleasure as it ebbs and he draws it out.

I'm so tired.

The performance, the drinks, the gushing orgasm. All of them combine to have my eyes unwilling to open after each slow blink. Soon, I'm snuggling deeper into William's embrace, promising myself I'll make him feel good when I wake. In the morning there will be time, and I'm going to give him the best damn blow job of his life. In my dream, I'm already picturing his rigid length and the veins I'll trace with my tongue before I suck him right into my mouth.

Of course when I wake in the gray morning light, he's gone. That's the worst thing about a gargoyle boyfriend. I can't believe I fell asleep on him like that. On the spare pillow there's an old-fashioned paper note. I don't even know where William found a pen or paper around here. They're certainly not things I'd have lying around.

When I open it, I take a few moments of squinting to figure out the curling script. When I do, I smile and press the note to my chest.

Princess,

Would not have woken you for the world. Sleep in. Stay warm. And do not walk through any more dark alleyways late at night or I may have to spank you again.

I grin, still feeling the phantom sting and resulting clench of pleasure after William's commanding treatment of my body last night.

Then I feel bad all over again that he didn't even get to come. God, I could wake up in his arms and slide beneath the blankets to wake him with my mouth around his already hard cock. I feel sure he'd snore, too, if he was a man and not a statue while he slept. Something about that thought brings another silly smirk to curve my lips.

I find my phone on the nightstand and flick on the screen. Twenty-one new messages. My smirk fades. Only one of them is from someone I know.

I swipe away the photo of me with three other cast members at the pub we visited last night, more intent on discovering what the other messages say. Reality is, I already know they're not good. I just have a sick feeling in my belly.

When I open the first one, I find I'm not wrong.

I hadn't checked my phone since I left the pub last night. A slew of messages from just after that and all the way through the morning have me swallowing down bitter bile.

PhatOne: Forgive me, sexy girl. I shouldn't have said those things last night. I'm just so jealous that so many other guys have felt that sweet little pussy wrapped around their cock and you've denied me that pleasure.

PhatOne: You blocked my other profile. I know, I know. I deserved it. But how am I supposed to apologize if you won't answer me?

PhatOne: You little bitch. Answer me.

PhatOne: What the fuck? I saw you with that monster. Saw you run into his arms like he's not some kind of abomination. Never picked you for a monster fucker.

Unable to read any more, I toss my phone face down onto the bed. My hands shake and a cold sweat has broken out on the back of my neck. Whoever this guy is, he was there in the alley last night, just like I thought. That's the only explanation for the timestamp on the ugly messages about William. It's the same guy who messaged me earlier. I know it.

I make myself pick the phone up and block the new account without reading any more messages. Then I take a shower hot enough to melt the skin off my bones and scrub myself with my loofa until I feel almost clean.

By the time I'm dressed, sipping a coffee with my feet tucked under me on a stool at the kitchen counter, Maurice emerges from his room down the hall. I hear him whistling before I see him. The sound lifts a little of the anxiety fog from my mind. Enough for me to give him a half smile, anyway.

Maurice yawns and stretches, scratching his belly before pouring himself a cup of coffee and leaning over the counter. "Rough night?"

I shake my head.

He gives me a long look, then shrugs and opens the fridge. "You eat yet?"

"Not hungry." Food is the last thing I want right now. What I want is to curl up in William's arms and close my eyes, and pretend the world will just disappear. But it's full daylight and he won't wake for hours yet.

"Suit yourself." He busies himself getting out eggs and bacon and setting a frypan on the stove. Without turning around, he says, "Show go well last night?"

"Yeah." I'd almost forgotten about the success of opening night. That makes me even more mad. This asshole doesn't have the right to shit all over one of the best things that's happened to me recently. "Yeah. It was great. In fact," I say, setting my mug down on the sink, "I'm going to head in for some early rehearsals before tonight's performance. I'll see you later tonight?"

"Sure." Maurice gives me a wave and cracks five eggs into the frypan. "Break a leg!"

There aren't really any rehearsals on today. In fact the cast have the day off. But I really want to see William, even if all I can do is sit near him and see if it helps make me feel better. I have a feeling the only thing that's going to settle my stomach today is his solid, reassuring presence.

So I brush my teeth and grab my bag, not bothering to change out of the sweats and sneakers I'm wearing around the house. No one will be there yet and when it's time for the show, I'll change into my costume. No way I'm going out after the show, either. Not tonight. Tonight, I'm letting William fly me straight back to the apartment, and I'm going to do my level best to convince him to stay so I can blow his bloody mind!

TWENTY TWO

Jessie

Sethos ambushes me as I'm about to open the door to William's tower. "Jessie, you're here early. Might I have a word?"

His tone is sly, like a fox which has spotted a mouse, but that's the way he always is. I brush it off and follow him back to Grande Lounge, on the level below the lobby. The theater is closed, so the lounge is empty, and we take a seat on two facing black leather sofas. I tuck my hands between my knees and try not to fidget. I'd much rather be on the tower with William, but I can't afford to piss off Sethos, not when he gave me a shot at the audition for this part when no other producer would consider me.

He regards me with his cat-like eyes and the tip of his tail twitches against the leg of the sofa. "Reviews for opening night have been outstanding."

I relax a little. Perhaps he just wants someone to listen to him gloat about how great his show is. I mean it is a great show and he should be proud. "That's wonderful. Then we'll do the extended run?" The original contract said the show might run for an extra three to six months, if the initial response was good.

Sethos nods. "I think we will, but that's not what I wanted to discuss with you."

I wait, hoping he's not about to say my performance was substandard.

"Almost all the reviews mention your solo," he says.

"It was brilliant. You are brilliant. I have to say you've been quite a find."

I'm temporarily speechless. This is not what I was expecting him to say. "T-thank you," I stammer and my palms are sweating though the news seems to be good.

"I'd like to draw up a new contract tying you to the Grand Theater. In exchange for exclusivity, I'll make sure you get lead roles in any production that goes on stage for the next five years. In fact, I've got a few things in mind that I think would suit your voice perfectly."

"Exclusivity? I'd have to think about that." I haven't even really considered other theaters, but locking myself in feels like a bit of a commitment.

Sethos nods. "As a token of my appreciation, I've arranged for you to have your own private dressing room. I'd like you to consider what I'm offering. Know that I will take very good care of you."

I nod, really just trying to take in his words. It's my dream come true. Lead roles, a long-term contract. Only it feels empty not having William here to talk to about it, knowing he'll be sleeping for hours yet. It will also mean a lot more exposure. That should be good. I've always accepted fame comes with success in this business. It's not like Hollywood. Not like the movies where you can't walk down the street without being recognized. But the nature of stage acting is means you perform for big crowds and if the show does well, your name and image are spread all over the city and beyond.

It's only after the creepy messages from last night and the day before, this suddenly feels a whole hell of a lot scarier than it ever did before.

Sethos is staring at me, waiting for an answer. I babble something about having my lawyer read over the contract. In reality, I haven't got a lawyer and he probably knows it, but he smiles and thanks me and lets me go dashing off to my dressing room to hide and collect my thoughts.

When I get there though, there's another surprise. A large bunch of roses sits in a pretty vase in the middle of my dressing table. I step out of the room and check the number on the door, but this is definitely my room. The one Sethos just told me was mine.

Frowning, I fumble with the flowers and search for a card. Probably someone left them here by mistake. What I see makes my guts churn.

A rose by any other name smells as sweet,
But a slut smells like a slut no matter how you dress her up.

I stuff the note into the trash and stagger from the dressing room with icy fingers and a roiling stomach. The cold wind on the east tower bites against my overheated cheeks as soon as I step out of the door.

William is on his perch looking down over the center stage. Perhaps it's my imagination, but tonight his shoulders look hunched and his features have an odd wistful look not normally there when I see him in daylight.

I wonder if he dreams while he sleeps, or if it's different under the curse. Coming close, I stretch up and brush a hand over his furrowed brow. Of course, it does nothing to smooth the worry lines etched there in stone. I can't even really hug him. His girth and the wings make it impossible for me to get my arms around him properly.

I sink to the ground and wrap my jacket more tightly around my body, huddling at his clawed feet. His marble beneath my thighs is cold, seeping through my sweats and chilling me the longer I sit. I don't move, though. I'm not ready to leave.

Neither do I open my mouth to tell him about Sethos's offer or the flowers and card in my dressing room. If I tell him now, he might remember, and knowing will only worry him. It's probably nothing. Just some creepy weirdo who'll get over it in a week or two. Surely, I can't be that fascinating to anyone that he can't find a new obsession to fixate on once the excitement of opening night dies down.

I tell myself this as the sun tips beyond its midday peak and gradually sinks toward the horizon. After a few hours, I reluctantly stretch and shake out my stiff, cold legs. I finally succumb to my growling stomach and descend from the tower to find something to eat. Then the busy rehearsals and preparations before the night's performance begin and I don't have to concentrate any longer on forgetting about it. I'm caught up in the whirlwind of excitement and I can finally switch off for a blissful few hours. When the show is over, William will be awake to protect me.

So I feel absolutely fine when I step into my dressing room and close the door behind me so I can begin putting on my costume.

TWENTY THREE

William

Something doesn't feel right tonight.

Jessie's performance is perfect. It's not that. For the second night in a row, the audience get to their feet to applaud her as her solo ends. For the second night in a row I gaze through the glass dome in awe at the way she gracefully accepts the accolades, then returns their attention to the performance, and seamlessly folds herself back into the scene.

She was born for this—to command attention and devotion. No wonder she literally woke me from stone.

I see her eyes flick to the ceiling, searching for me more than once during the show. When later, I knock quietly at her dressing room door and enter, she's in a strange mood.

"There you are!" She sets down the little towel she's using to remove her makeup and flings herself straight into my arms. I think nothing of it at first. She's always openly affectionate, brimming with life and laughter. Jessie stretches up for a kiss which turns hungry in an instant. Her tongue pushes at my lips and tangles with mine. Her little moans of pleasure speed my pulse and in moments, she's wrapping her legs around my hips, climbing me, clinging to me.

I can't say I'm complaining. After last night, my balls are aching to come. Her breathy cries and salty sweet juices are still fresh in my mind. Pretty soon, my cock is hard and straining between us and I shove things from the dressing table onto the floor so I can set her down and pull her hips forward to grind myself against her wet heat.

Christ, she's wearing only panties beneath the thin silky gown that's already half undone. The barrier of black fabric is already damp and perfumed with her arousal.

GIVEN TO THE GARGOYLE

A vase of flowers teeters at the edge of the counter and I snatch it before it can smash on the floor. Jessie looks around and something closes across her eyes like a blind being lowered. She frowns and turns her face away from my next kiss. "Take me home."

"Mmm," I murmur against her neck, not willing to take my mouth from her flesh even for a moment. "Later."

She stiffens. "Now. Please. Let's go home."

Pulling back, I cup her face with my hands and study her expression. "What is it, princess?"

Her hands cover mine, but she won't meet my eyes. "Nothing."

It clearly isn't nothing, but if something has spooked her, perhaps being at home is exactly what she needs. With a sigh and a final kiss, I drag myself from the cradle of her thighs and palm down my throbbing erection. It can wait. I can wait, until I have her all to myself, relaxed and happy and sated. Then and only then will I allow myself the pleasure of sinking into her sweet channel and taking what I so desperately need.

We gather her things. Jessie pulls on her jeans and sweater, pulling her warm jacket and scarf over the top of everything else. Then we turn to go.

"You want to take your flowers, angel?"

She shakes her head. "No."

She doesn't explain further and I don't press her. I walk her to the door of the theater and gather her up in my arms the moment we're outside.

I'm not a monster—well I am, but I really do intend to take things slow and talk to her about what's bothering her once we get back to her apartment. No sooner have I hunched over to duck through the door though, and Jessie slips out of my arms and drops to her knees on the carpet.

"Jessie—"

"Shhh. Maurice is working tonight and you let me fall asleep last night without getting you off."

"You don't have to—" I break off with a strangled noise when she tugs aside my loincloth and takes my cock in her small hand. Christ! It's already throbbing and weeping just at the sight of her down there. She gives me a wicked grin then flattens her tongue and runs it right up the base of my shaft.

Fuck me! That's all it takes.

My hand strays to her long hair and she moans when I thread my claws into the silky strands. Her tongue continues the torment, lapping at my flesh in long slow strokes that have me weak at the knees. When she reaches the point right beneath the head, I groan and my fingers tighten in her hair.

She huffs a tiny cruel laugh and flicks that spot with the tip of her tongue. I nearly crack in half with pleasure.

"By the virgin, you are a wicked woman. Don't stop."

The smile at the corners of her lips is unmistakable as she blinks up at me through impossibly long lashes. Then she opens her mouth and takes the whole of my cockhead into that sweet wet heat and I'm utterly lost.

One gentle hand cups my sac and draws carefully at my tight bollocks, massaging them until my breath is ragged and my wings unfurl. God I love the things she does to me with her pretty mouth!

There's a crash. Something tips from a bookshelf onto the floor. Jessie giggles. Her mouth leaves my cock with a wet pop and I groan. "Tonight you're mine to do exactly what I want with."

I grunt. "I'm yours." Doesn't she know the power she wields?

She continues, stroking me leisurely with her hand. "What I want tonight is to make you come harder than you've ever come in your life."

She gets to her feet and I nearly beg for her mouth on me again, but she plants her small hands in the center of my chest and gives me a shove. "On my bed, William. Naked and waiting for me."

I don't hesitate to follow her instructions.

My tiny fierce princess follows me slowly. I watch her slip the jacket over her shoulders and toss it onto a chair. Then she pulls her sweater over her head as she reaches the doorway.

When she enters the room, she slows down further. She toes off her shoes and lets down her long hair from the knot on top of her head. The rich brown strands fall over her shoulders, catch the light and give off glints of red and gold.

She slides her hands beneath her cotton shirt, lifting the fabric and teasing over her taut belly. Her navel piercing glitters, but I'm far more absorbed with the way she lets me see just the bottom of her breasts. It's just enough to remind me she still has on no bra to restrict them. As if I could forget. Her hard nipples strain at the thin fabric and I swallow, longing to have my mouth on them, waiting for her to do what she will to me.

She stalks closer and slips the jeans over her hips. She stops to remove them, leaving her in only the small top and the lacy black panties I know are damp between her thighs.

I'm lying on my back as she commanded me, propping myself on my elbows to watch her. When she climbs into my lap, straddling my hips, I slump back with a sigh, but she doesn't give me any relief. Not yet.

My cock juts out from my body, twitching with her every movement. Even without her touch, I'm throbbing. Jessie moves sensuously, running her hands up and down her legs, rolling her hips and her body, but never bringing her sweet pussy quite close enough.

Finally, she pulls the top over her head and her glorious breasts spill from beneath it. She lifts them and toys with the nipples, moaning aloud for me to hear as my cock grows impossibly harder.

God's blood, she'll kill me with anticipation. Her wicked hands slide up and down her belly, grazing her mound, teasing me. "Woman, if your hands aren't on that slick little pussy soon, then my mouth will be."

She laughs, but pushes her hands beneath the tiny black panties. I groan as her perfume swells. My mouth waters. Jessie moans and I can't take my eyes from the movement of her fingers as she plays with herself.

"You'd like that, wouldn't you? But tonight is about you. About me making you feel good."

I growl. "I could have sworn it was about you tormenting me. Get over here."

She only lifts a finger to shake it in my face. "No, no. You just lay back and relax."

"Relax? Does any part of me look relaxed to you?" I gesture down at my body, every part strained and taut and eager for her.

Jessie grins. "Mmm, let me take care of that for you." She slides off me, slips off the panties and tosses them at my face. The smell of the damp fabric alone makes my balls tighten, so I almost miss when she climbs back on top and her naked pussy descends right over my poor aching cock.

She still doesn't take pity on me, though. Jessie plants her hands on my chest and rides me without ever letting me inside. I groan as each roll of her hips paints my cock with her juices, yet never once gives me what I crave.

She leans over me. My body is so sensitive the brush of her long hair across my skin is like a lash. Soft lips and wet tongue flick a tantalizing path along my collarbone and down to my nipple. "Will you tell me when you're about to come?"

My laugh is pained. "Woman, I'd come at your command. You want me to come for you?" My sac tightens and liquid pleasure courses along my shaft.

"Not yet." She bites down on my nipple. I give a strangled cry.

"I want you to wait. Can you do that?"

I growl through gritted teeth. "As you wish."

Finally she reaches between us and guides my throbbing dick inside her. It's almost worse than before. She slides onto me with such agonizing care that I'm shaking by the time her cunny swallows the last inch. We both sigh and I can't help grabbing her waist to thrust up into her just once. "Fuck!" I breathe the curse and she laughs, nodding.

"I know."

Her lips part when I do it again. Pride swells my chest at the slightly dazed look that crosses her face. "Again."

I hold her steady and lift my hips to plunge in and out of her.

Jessie groans. "Fuck me. Just like that."

What can I do but obey my princess?

I grip her hips, half scared I'll pierce her tender flesh with my claws, but too lost to stop. I lift up, sinking my cock in and out of her cunny, rewarded by the erotic sounds of our joining. Pleasure spears me, stealing thought and leaving me with only sensation.

She's so tight. Her pussy is so wet it accepts me easily, but each time I withdraw, she grips me like she never wants me to leave. Only the bliss of leaving her body in order to thrust in deeper is better than anything.

Jessie gasps as I rock her body with the force of my punishing thrusts. Each time I push up into her, I use my grip to bring her down, lifting her again as I withdraw.

I growl. My tail coils around her waist to hold her firmly. Dirty words spew from my mouth. "So good. So fucking good. Your hungry little cunny takes me so good."

"Are you close?"

"Yes." I'm reluctant to admit it, but she's had me ready to spill since she put her mouth on me.

"Stop."

Gritting my teeth, I obey her command. Then Jessie begins to move. It's a new sensation. She's not lifting up and down, but grinding against me, using me for her pleasure. "Don't come," she warns.

Saints in heaven, she asks the impossible. If it was anyone else I'd laugh in their face, but Jessie's pleasure is my prize, so I nod. "I won't come."

Sucking her lower lip between her teeth, she lifts one hand from my chest and brings it to her clit. I feel it as soon as she begins rubbing. Her cunt tightens and flutters around my cock. I'm barely holding on.

"Don't come." She chides. "I want you to feel me come around your cock. Then you're going to fill me up so full it's dripping from me for days."

I let out an involuntary cry as her words fill my mind with filthy images. I hold back when she rocks her hips. I hold back when she clenches and tips her head back, moaning my name. Somehow, I even hold back when she stops coming and looks down at me with such a flushed and rosy-cheeked expression I can practically feel how good her orgasm was.

Finally, she climbs off me and rolls to her back on the bed, lifting her legs to spread herself out for me. "Fill me up, babe. Give it to me."

I'm on top of her in a heartbeat, even moving as slowly as I'm able. I push my cock back into her tight sheath and groan at the sight of her swallowing me up. At this angle, she's impossibly tight and I know I don't have long left in me.

I brace myself on one hand and begin to thrust. My other hand slips between us to find Jessie's swollen clit. I know I've found just the right place when she gasps and clenches.

"That's right, princess. You going to come again for me? Come as I fill you up?"

She moans, nodding and biting her lip.

I work her faster, increasing the speed of my thrusts until I'm hanging by a thread.

Jessie lets out a keening cry. She spasms. I can't hold back any longer.

I grunt and snap my hips forward, burying myself right to the hilt. Pleasure shoots up my spine, blacks my vision, and empties my bollocks deep, deep inside my girl.

My knot swells and her cries grow louder. I have a moment's worry, until I see her face, flushed and open-mouthed with bliss, pressed back against the pillows. Then I give myself over to it and let the feeling spread.

She holds me close and I marvel how lucky I am. It's not just sexual release. It sounds foolish, but it feels spiritual. Like a draining of negative thoughts and negative energy. What replaces them is more beautiful, more profound than I have words for.

I simply stroke her hair back from her brow and press a kiss there while we're still joined. "My princess. My love."

I wish I had better words, but I can only give her what I have. Until now, I've felt unworthy, inept. Yet tonight, I let go of that for just a moment, surrendering myself to her and to my feelings. I'll offer myself to her. Offer her everything I have, everything I am. And my princess will decide if I'm enough. One way or another, I won't have to worry about it anymore.

TWENTY
FOUR

Jessie

Over the next three nights, no messages and no flowers arrive. Nothing. I still make sure William takes me home straight after the curtain call each night. I don't mention my fears. Instead, I make sure to wear myself out coming so many times on his cock I drift easily into a peaceful sleep with no dreams of lurking strangers in the dark or foul breath on the back of my neck.

By the end of the week, I've relaxed enough to stop searching the crowd for sinister faces, and no longer get the sick feeling in the pit of my stomach every time I look at my phone. A firm rap on my dressing room door still makes me jump, though. Tugging on my dressing gown, I open the door to find Sethos there. He glares over my shoulder, tail flicking his leg. "Where's that good-for-nothing gargoyle? I swear he's never here when I want to talk to him."

I fold my arms over my chest. "Not like you actually pay him or anything."

He hisses and flicks his large feathered wings. "What would a gargoyle do with money anyway?"

"Why don't you ask him? But as far as I'm concerned, supernaturals deserve the same rights as humans, working conditions included. I'm pretty sure the local council would agree."

"Listen. Have you seen him or not? There's been a very serious threat made, so if you know where he is, then tell him to come find me. And if there's an alarm, for gods' sake, evacuate quickly."

Chilling proclamation made, he turns and stalks away down the corridor. I tuck the gown tighter around me and close the door. Truth is, I don't know where William is. I assumed he was on the roof where he typically stations himself during a show. Sethos isn't stupid, though, as annoying as he is. So I'm sure he's looked there.

William has an unerring ability to find me when I want him to. Sethos' concern worries me. On the stool in front of my mirror, I debate with myself. Whatever this is doesn't sound like it's targeted at me. The sooner I find William so Sethos can fill him in, the safer everyone will be.

Opening the door again, I peek out into the corridor.

There's no one around.

I only make it halfway to the east tower stairs before a guy in black dress pants and a black collared shirt enters from the door to the foyer. He frowns. "Miss Jessie, you should be in your changing room until Mr. Issa gives the all clear. Didn't you hear there was a bomb threat?"

I don't recognize him. I open my mouth to reply that I'm looking for William, but he strides toward me and takes my arm. "Hey!"

I struggle, but he's too strong. Something about his face is familiar, but I can't place it. It doesn't help that he has a cap pulled down over his head. He turns me back in the direction of my dressing room. "Back this way, miss. You'd better let me check the room while I'm here. Make sure you're safe."

"Who are you? What's going on?"

He opens the door, guides me inside, and closes the door behind us. Now we're alone, a terrible oily sick feeling slides over my skin, but the guy releases me. I take another look at his face, which seems familiar, but I can't place him.

"Mr. Issa hired extra security for the next few weeks. Lucky he did. If you just relax and do what I say, we'll have the building cleared and we'll be ready to get on with the show."

He looks around the room, lifting items on the floor and running his fingers along the skirting board. I don't like the way he just manhandled me, but his actions aren't those of someone who wants to do me harm.

The security guard reaches under my dressing table. "You've been in this room since five, miss?"

I nod.

"And no one else came in here?"

"No. Not unless you count Sethos."

The guy snorts. He picks my handbag up and slides a hand inside, setting it back down again when he fails to find whatever he's looking for. Then he straightens. "Looks like you're all good here. Just hang tight, and someone will let you know when it's safe to move around the building again."

He goes to the door and lets himself out. I continue processing what's just happened. Reaching for my phone, I see it's already past the half hour and I should have checked in with the director five minutes ago.

Nothing for it.

With a clinging sense of worry, I apply the last of my makeup and throw on my costume. Tucking my hair beneath my wig cap, I pull the wig on top. One of my fellow cast members can help check if it's on straight, but I can't afford to delay any more. I drop my phone into my handbag and hurry backstage.

GIVEN TO THE GARGOYLE

It's only after the show wraps and the curtain falls I start to wonder why I still haven't seen William. I haven't seen any more of the extra security guys either, come to think of it.

I hurry back to my dressing room and do a speedy change into my sweats, snatch up my handbag and head to the east tower. When I get up there, the archway is empty with no sign of my big gargoyle.

The skin at the back of my neck prickles and gooseflesh raises on the backs of my arms. Suddenly I don't want to stay here a moment longer. I take extra care when I leave the Grande. Instead of walking, I hail a cab and pay for the security of a locked car cabin for the two and a half blocks or so I'd normally walk.

See, William. I listen.

I half expect him to be waiting for me when I unlock the door and walk through into the living room. But the balcony is empty. The sensor light is off and the apartment is cold and dark.

I go through the place, flicking on all the lights, turning up the heater too high and setting the shower to the hottest temperature. Stripping off, I scald my skin under the hot water and step out into a room thick with steam. As I open the bathroom door, the steam escapes in a billow, rushing past me and clouding my vision for a fraction of a moment. Just enough to make me doubt movement by the front door.

"Maurice?" I call out, even though I know my roommate is working late tonight.

There's no answer.

Did I lock the front door? I was in such a rush to see if William was waiting on the balcony I'm not sure.

The prickling feeling at the back of my neck is back. A horribly familiar voice from my bedroom door makes my stomach drop through the floor.

"You're mine now, you filthy little slut. Now you're going to give me what you owe me."

The security guard from the theater is in my apartment. Only now I realize he's not a guard at all. And I know where I've seen that dimpled chin before.

As he advances, I stumble back against the bed. I can't believe I let him get me. I'm not going to let this happen without a fight, though.

TWENTY
FIVE

William

I shouldn't be here. I shift from foot to clawed foot as the guy behind the counter takes out a magnifying glass and inspects my coins. He sniffs, flipping one over and pushing it further beneath the spotlight he has on it.

"They'll be tricky to sell. Takes a real specialist to be interested in stuff like this. They might sit here for years."

I sigh. It's more or less the same thing the last three guys told me. None of them gave me a price anywhere near what I'll need to make any difference to Jessie's savings. I was hoping I'd at least be able to afford a deposit on an apartment, but I'm at least ten thousand short of what I'd need for even that.

"Well?" He drops the glass onto the counter and looks at me. "What do you wanna do?"

I curl my claws into a fist. This should be simple. It's not like I have a better choice.

"Let me think about it. I'll come back tomorrow."

The pawn shop owner sniffs again. "Suit yourself."

Scooping my coins off the counter, I return them to the frayed leather bag and hurry outside. I've gone further from the theater than I wanted, searching for one more place in the hopes this guy would give me a better offer. I'm going to miss the curtain call if I don't hurry. I should have been there for the whole show, but this was more important. If I'd waited until later, the shops would have been closed. I found that out the hard way.

When I make it back, I know immediately I chose the wrong night for my little excursion. A fuming Sethos is stalking the east tower when I land. "Where were you?"

"I had business to attend to," I grumble. In reality, I'm already feeling guilty for not being here. Immediately, I head toward the stairs, intent on finding Jessie. Sethos steps into my way. "Not so fast. You gave me your word. I know the terms of the curse. If you want to wake again tomorrow night, you had better stop and listen."

"Or what? You'll freeze me and be completely without a guard? What good will that do?" I fold my arms across my chest and glare down at him.

"It's not doing me much good right now having a guard who's not here when I need him. Did you know we had a bomb threat tonight? Of course, you don't. You weren't here!"

I stare. "A what?"

"A bomb threat. Some maniac rang and threatened to blow up the whole place. Lucky I decided not to call the police in the end, since it turned out to be nothing. If I'd have called, they'd have shut down my theater for days. As it was, some of the cast were spooked. The performance suffered."

"You didn't call police?" I can't believe what I'm hearing. "What if it had been genuine? What if the whole place was destroyed?"

Sethos shrugs. "It wasn't. If you had been here we could have established that a lot sooner."

I cut through the air and his words with a slice of my hand. "Where's Jessie?"

Sethos snorts. "Your precious human is fine. She went home already."

"I'll be the judge of that." I push past him, brushing him aside like he's not even there.

Sethos growls. "I'm warning you, du Buisson—"

I turn back with a roar. Sethos darts out of my way, but I'm not interested in him. I'm interested in getting to my mate and establishing she is unharmed. Stalking to my perch, I bend and tear it from the stone floor. Sethos curses and I ignore him.

"I hereby give you my resignation." Giving him a mock salute, I tuck the stone perch under my arm and leap from the tower.

He calls after me, but I ignore him. Spreading my wings, I catch a warm updraft from the sewerage system below and let it lift me higher. Sethos could follow, but he doesn't. Clearly, he knows when he's lost an argument.

I put him out of my mind and focus all my senses on the streets below and on my destination. In a matter of moments, I'm landing with a crunch on Jessie's balcony. All the lights are on, but when I try the door, it's locked, though she normally leaves it open for me. That in itself makes my tail flick. I hear muffled sounds through the glass and let out an angry roar.

I don't bother trying the door again. I just put my fist and elbow straight through it. Glass crashes. More shouts come from within the apartment.

Jessie cries, "William!"

I lose my fucking mind.

Shards crunch beneath my rough soles as I storm through the living room, knocking aside furniture in my rush. I drop the stone perch with a thunk and race toward my woman. I tear her bedroom door from its hinges with the force of my anger and drop the broken wood to the floor as I take in the scene in front of me.

Jessie cowers on the floor, completely naked. Tears streaming down her cheeks and red marks around her wrists and across her face tell me everything I need to know about what's happening here.

Beside the bed, a man fumbles with the front of his trousers, tucking himself away as if that will somehow stop me from removing his fucking prick from his body before I slowly disembowel him.

My voice is dark, deeper than even I thought possible when I speak. "How slowly should I kill this miserable sack of shit?"

Jessie's answer is a pained whimper. The guy is hardly more articulate. "D-don't kill me." He's stumbling around the room, avoiding my claws as I swipe at him.

I dive for him, but he ducks beneath my arm and scrambles for the door. Not a fucking chance. I round on him, snatching his ankle and smiling cruelly when he slams to the floor, his chin making a resounding thud on the floorboards.

The asshole curses as I drag him back through the door and lift him off his feet. He doesn't have the breath left for cursing, though, when I smash him against the wall, my hand on the back of his neck.

"William!"

With my free hand, I gather the guy's wrist and twist it up behind him until he wails. "Did you touch her?"

"William!"

"Did you fucking touch her?"

"No!" The man's words are muffled and distorted since his face is pressed against the wall.

"Did you?"

"No, I said. Little bitch thinks she's too good to suck my cock."

"She doesn't think she's too good, asshole. She knows she is. She's too good to piss on your burning corpse."

"William!" Finally, Jessie's high pitched cries break through the icy rage that frosts my skin, numbing me to anything but this asshole's pain.

"William, don't."

I stop and draw in a long breath through my nostrils. My princess tells me to stop and I listen. Everything in me still screams to begin his true suffering.

"You can't."

"Oh, I can. It will be my pleasure," I assure her.

The man whimpers.

Her touch feathers over my back between my wings. "No. You can't. Because I don't know what the authorities will do to you if you do. And I need you."

The words choke the air from my lungs. It's me who needs her. Desperately. But if there's even a chance Jessie feels the way I feel, then I'm not doing anything to jeopardize it.

"You do?" I drop the intruder, who collapses to his knees. Turning to face Jessie, I reach for her but hesitate.

She doesn't. She flings herself against my chest as if I haven't been about to tear a man apart with my bare hands like some twisted golem, operating on automatic. "You're here."

I place a shaking hand atop her head. "I'm here."

"Just when I needed you."

"Too late!" I curse myself for the delay. For not being here earlier.

Jessie shakes her head against my body. "No. You're here."

A crunch of broken glass from the living room alerts me just in time.

I curse. "Fucker." Releasing Jessie quickly, I storm after her attacker and grab him by the back of his jacket just as he is sneaking out.

"If you want to call police, Jessie, then do it now while I still have some measure of control. If this asshole so much as looks at you the wrong way again, I can't guarantee he'll survive until they get here."

Jessie fumbles for her phone in her handbag and I throw the man down onto the floor, standing over him. Folding my arms across my chest keeps me from wrapping my hands around his throat.

I don't even really listen to her phone call. Instead, all my focus is on reminding myself Jessie doesn't want me to kill him. She told me not to kill him.

It's shameful, but I still spend the next few minutes imagining all the ways I'd like to.

I try not to imagine the things he might have done to Jessie if I had been only a moment later. If I had stayed and accepted the offer from the pawn shop owner. If I had listened to Sethos a minute longer.

Thank heavens, I didn't.

Finally, I look around me at Jessie. She's thrown on an old shirt and is sweeping broken glass from what remains of Maurice's living room and I realize I might have managed not to kill her attacker, but I've still made a hash of just about everything else.

TWENTY
SIX

GIVEN TO THE GARGOYLE

William

As soon as the police officer finishes taking Jessie's statement and clears out, leaving us alone in the apartment, I scoop her off her feet.

She laughs. "Where are you taking me?"

I stride straight down the corridor and pull back the bedcover with a clawed foot. Depositing her into bed, I pull them over her and tuck her in.

"There's still so much cleaning up to do before Maurice gets home. I can't go to bed yet."

"I got it."

She starts to push back the covers and I let out a low growl. She raises her hands and laughs. "OK, OK. I'm not going to fight you. You sure you don't want me to help?" Her offer is spoiled when she lets out a long yawn.

I shake my head. "Of course not. It's my fault. I will clear it up."

"Aw, thanks, babe. I'm really beat."

"Lay back. Relax. Try to get some sleep."

She nods and smothers another yawn.

I stalk back into the living room and survey the damage. Glass is everywhere, all over the floor by the balcony and a large pile is beneath the low table that holds the television. The night breeze blows in through the smashed door. I close the blinds, but it does little to keep out the chill. I should call someone to replace the door, but when I find Jessie's phone on the sofa, I can't even make the screen move beyond the photo of us she insisted on putting as her 'wallpaper'. It took her a long time to explain to me she wasn't pasting it onto the walls of her house, but capturing a tiny image to put on her phone. Sometimes I don't know why she bothers with someone as dense as me.

Shaking my head, I carefully place the phone back onto the table and get to work on the glass. That, at least, I can do. When the glass is swept, I straighten the furniture and glance down at my stone perch in the middle of the living room. I can't believe I didn't think of it sooner. Removing my perch to Jessie's apartment means I only have to go as far as the balcony by morning. I can be here when she wakes up, even though I'll be sleeping by then. I hope that will mean something.

She calls to me from the bedroom. "Babe? Can you make me a cup of tea? I can't sleep."

"Of course."

In the kitchen, I spend a long moment staring at all the cupboards and little electronic devices. I have no idea how to operate most of them. It feels like a triumph when I locate the tea at the top of the pantry and a cup and set them on the counter. Now I just need hot water. I rummage around until I find a metal pan the size I want and fill it with water from the faucet. But the stove absolutely stumps me. I'm quietly cursing, turning the knobs back and forward, thinking to myself that the overwhelming smell of gas cannot be a good thing, when I hear a quiet chuckle from behind me. I spin. Jessie is leaning against the refrigerator laughing at me. "Babe, what are you doing?"

"Making you tea." My tone is more sullen than I have any right to. She doesn't deserve my ire.

She slips her arms around my waist and leans her cheek between my wings. "That's what the kettle is for. Let me show you." She marches straight to a metal jug on the counter and flicks a switch. Immediately some modern witchcraft ignites a fire under it and I hear the whir of water beginning to heat.

God damn me, why am I so useless?

Just then the front door opens and Maurice takes approximately two and a half steps into the apartment I thought I had cleaned. He stops and whistles. "You two either had a really good night or a really bad one. What did I miss?"

I hang my head. "You mean the part where I smashed your door or the part where I was nearly too late to save Jessie from being assaulted?"

They both stare at me for a heartbeat. Then Jessie shakes her head. "The part where you did save me, babe. Where you were my absolute hero and then you cleaned up all the mess while I lay in bed and you tried to make me tea."

"I couldn't," I mumble.

Maurice throws down his phone on the counter and leans against it. "Everyone alright?"

Jessie nods. "I'm fine now. Thanks to William. The cops came and arrested the guy and I've made a statement. Seems like he'll be under surveillance until the hearing."

Maurice nods. "How did he get in?"

Jessie shifts and I realize I didn't even ask. Did I mention I'm a fool?

"I think he followed me home from the theater."

I was too busy fuming and standing guard when she gave her statement to the police, but now I'm all ears. "He what?"

"It was the same guy from the function. The one who spat on me. The police think he put a tracker in my handbag."

"That bastard!" My wings spread and I grip the counter hard enough I hope to God I don't break off a chunk. "I knew I should have killed him."

Jessie's small hand covers mine. "No. I'm glad you didn't. Remember what I said? I need you."

I shake my head. "Don't know why. What kind of man isn't there for his woman when she needs him?"

Jessie scoffs. "You were. But that reminds me, where were you tonight? I didn't see you at the show. And what with the bomb threat and everything... well, I guess that was all part of that guy stalking me, now I think about it. But where were you?"

I sigh and push back from the counter, walking to the table where I left my leather pouch of coins. Bringing them back to the kitchen, I tip them onto the counter. "On a fool's errand. I tried to sell these, to see if I could make enough money to at least provide a place for you to live. Turns out I'm useless in that as well."

Maurice leans over the counter and makes another low whistle. "How much were you selling them for?"

I look at him, puzzled. "I thought I might be able to get ten thousand. Turns out they're not even worth half that."

He barks a laugh and I twist to look at him more closely.

"Ah, I think they could be worth a hell of a lot more than ten grand, brother. Are these what I think they are?"

I shrug. "What do you think they are?"

"Original eleventh century French deniers?"

I scratch the back of my head. "I guess so. They're just my savings. From when I was human."

Maurice shakes his head. "To the right buyer these are worth a fortune."

I stare at him. "They are?"

He nods. "They are. I think. I'm no coins expert. But I know a guy. Want me to ask him?"

I place my hand on his shoulder and bow my head. "My friend, I already owe you a far larger debt than I can ever repay for giving Jessie a place to stay when I couldn't, and for helping me find her when we did. But this—" I break off, throat tight and voice thin.

"It's nothing. I'll do it in the morning. You know she can stay, right? I like having company. It gets lonely with no pack and no mate. I'd ask you to stay as well, but you can't, can you?"

I make a long drawn out sound. "Ahhh, about that..."

Maurice perks up. "Yes?"

"I may have torn my perch from the roof of the theater in an argument with Sethos. So if you don't mind very much, I was hoping to leave it on your balcony, just for a while."

He grins. "Say no more! And don't be in a rush to leave."

Jessie flings herself into my side. "You're staying?"

I nod. "I guess I'm staying. Sort of. I'll still have to return to my perch at first light."

She squeezes tighter. "I don't care. That's the best news ever."

I shake my head but put my arm around her and hold her tight. "I'm glad you think so, princess. But I will work on finding us a place eventually. And a job. I need a job."

"We could always use more security at Monstrous Deals," Maurice says.

I nod, silently wondering how all the problems that seemed so big at the start of the night, have somehow become so small. If only there was a way to break the curse, my world would be just about perfect right now.

TWENTY
SEVEN

Jessie

"Great job, everyone. That's a wrap for today. Don't forget the rehearsal schedule ramps up next week ahead of opening night on Saturday." The director stands from his seat in the audience and applauds us as we break out of character and turn and walk offstage, smiling and congratulating each other.

On the way to my dressing room, Ashley squeezes my arm. "Oh my god. Have I told you enough times how amazing your voice is?"

I laugh. She tells me this every time we rehearse. I have to say I'm still not tired of hearing it. This part feels like it was freaking made for me. I'm half-convinced it was. I've never seen the show anywhere else and Sethos wouldn't tell us where he got the script.

Glancing at my phone after I'm changed, I frown. Still at least three hours until sunset. It's funny. I used to love summer, but the longer hours of daylight mean fewer hours with William. I can't say I'm loving that.

Might as well stop in and see if Sethos is hanging around. I've been meaning to talk to him.

I'm pleased when I spot the sphinx in the VIP box with his phone to his ear. He turns, spotting me, and raises a finger to signal me to wait. I could roll my eyes, but it won't make him any less arrogant, so I just wait. I can let him boss me around a bit until I ask him the favor I want to ask him.

A few minutes later, he opens the glass door and ushers me in. "Miss Jessie. What can I do for my shining star?"

I snort. "I'm glad you asked, actually. There is something you can do for me."

He sighs dramatically, but a smile plays at the corner of his mouth. I'm clearly in the good books this week. "Do go on."

"I want you to tell me how to break the curse."

Sethos lifts a manicured brow. "And what curse would that be?"

I fold my arms across my chest. "The gargoyle curse."

He gives me a long look, his cat-like eyes unblinking. "What makes you think I know anything about that?"

"Oh, come on. You knew about everything else. How to reverse the petrifaction, about the mates thing. You do know, don't you?"

"Perhaps. What's it worth to you?"

I knew it would come to this. I'm not mucking around though, so I lead with my best and only bargaining chip. "Your exclusivity contract."

"Go on."

"I'll sign your contract, if you tell me how to lift the curse from William."

Sethos' tail flicks against the arm of the red velvet sofa. "Agreed. I'll have my solicitor draw up the amended contract tomorrow."

I wait.

"Anything else?" He smirks.

"Aren't you going to tell me now?"

"Oh no. First you sign. Then I tell. That's how this works."

I scowl at him. "No. First you tell. Then I sign. Or no deal." I stand, ready to walk out. My heart is thumping in my chest, but I keep my hands steady. It's all acting. Just have to keep my cool and hope he breaks first. Sethos says nothing, so I turn and gather up my handbag, striding toward the door.

He growls. "Fine. Sit down. Sit down. I'll tell you."

William

I open my eyes and immediately regret it. Someone is shining a blinding light at my face. The glare is excruciating. It's brighter than any stage light or neon light.

Groaning, I shield my eyes with my hand and blink through my fingers at the blue sky.

Blue!

Sunlight!

It's been centuries since I've seen full daylight, but as soon as it occurs to me I realize that's what this is. But how?

I grip the rail of the balcony and stare at the city below, marveling at how the sunlight glints off car windshields and warms my skin. God's blood, I've missed this. Not even going to the cinema with Jessie and watching sunlight on the big screen compares. Nothing could.

But what does it mean?

Turning, I push open the door to the living room and search until I find the old phone she gave me. I fumble with the tiny thing for a few moments, finally managing to switch on the screen. "Siri, call princess."

The phone beeps. "The formal way to address a princess is Your Royal Highness. All subsequent—"

"No, you stupid bloody thing. Call princess!"

Another beep. "Calling Prince's Palace restaurant."

"By the blood of the virgin, you stupid fucking thing! Call Jessie!"

A buzzing noise from behind me makes me whip around. Jessie is leaning against the doorframe. She has a smirk on her pretty face and holds her ringing phone in one hand. "You're getting better, babe. Only three tries that time."

I can't stay angry when she directs her killer smile at me and drops her things to run and jump into my arms. Her mouth is on mine and her legs wrap around my hips before I can get out any words. For a few minutes, I'm completely distracted.

Then she breaks away. "It worked!"

I press my forehead against hers and pull together my scrambled thoughts. "It did?" Then my brain catches up. "What did you do?"

She pulls back and grins at me. "Broke the curse."

I stare. "How?" My heart is thundering in my chest and my wings extend, threatening to knock several things off the coffee table. If she broke the curse, why do I still look like this? "Are you sure? Look at me." I shouldn't be so ungrateful. I'm lucky even to have found a woman like Jessie.

Jessie brushes my cheek with her palm. "I'm kinda glad it didn't change the way you look, actually. I was worried you'd look different."

"You were?"

She leans in and presses a soft kiss to my lips. "I like you just like this. I hope you don't mind, though. Do you miss being human?"

I sit back on the sofa with an oomph when my legs give out under me. She *likes* the way I am now? "Princess, I'd be happy being a frog if it made *you* happy."

She giggles. "Let's stay with gargoyle, OK?"

I nod. "Deal."

I slide my hands over her waist and down to the juicy ass I love so much. Jessie makes a little hum and grinds in closer. Then I stop. "How did you do it?"

"Do what?"

"Break the curse."

"Oh! Well first I made Sethos tell me what to do."

I lift a brow. "What did you have to do to get him to do that?"

She laughs. "I signed a contract to say I'd give Grand Theater first option to hire me for all upcoming shows for the next five years."

I suck in a breath. "You sure that was wise?"

"Well, I figure Sethos wants to cast me in the leading role, then I'll happily work at Grande. Besides, I don't want to perform at a theater you don't guard. As long as you're happy to keep working there, of course."

I grin. "A paid job with the best view in town? You better believe I'm not going anywhere else, angel."

"See, so it wasn't a bad idea."

"But how did you do it?" I insist.

She grins. "I returned the ring. Took me about a month to track down the family it belonged to. Maurice's buddy, the antique dealer, helped me out, and we found it. Then I contacted them online, to say I'd send it back if they wanted it. The tracked package arrived today." She spreads her hands out and her grin grows wider. "And here we are."

I gather her close and pepper kisses along her jaw and neck, then all over her face. "Fucking genius. So that's it? I'm not trapped on my plinth during the day? I can sleep when you sleep and wake when you wake?"

She nods. "Sethos thinks so. Unless the family re-issue the curse, but they'd have to know the right spell."

I make the sign of the cross over me. It's funny what old superstitious habits come back to me at the strangest moments. I'm not taking any chances, though. "Let's pray that never happens."

"Mmm. Hey, you wanna find out if anything else is different? Are you hungry?"

I consider her question. I haven't eaten in nearly one thousand years. Food can wait. I am starved for something, though. I smile. "I could eat."

Jessie makes to get up from my lap and I pull her back down with a low growl.

"I could eat, I said. I didn't mean food."

She laughs. "Oh! Well in that case, maybe we should test out if that's different first, huh?"

I let a low rumble vibrate my chest. "We might have to test it more than once. I'm suddenly feeling a powerful need to please you."

She moans while I trail kisses down her neck and over the swell of her gorgeous tits. Then she lifts up on her knees and pulls up the fitted skirt she's wearing, exposing a hint of lacy black panties. My cock stands completely to attention in an instant.

"God, I wish you could watch yourself as I take you," I groan into her chest. "You're the most beautiful thing in this world when you come for me."

"Mmm. I think we could work something out." She pulls away. For a moment, I don't understand. Then she takes my hand and leads me into her bedroom. Pushing me down to sit on the foot of the bed, she turns so she's facing away from me, looking right at the floor to ceiling mirror on the sliding door of her wardrobe. Oh, this woman!

I push the skirt up further, exposing those tiny panties, cut to sit high over the perfect globes of her rounded ass. She looks so fucking delicious I can't help myself. Leaning in, I bite gently into the swell of her flesh until she gasps. Then we're both tearing at her clothes, in a rush to get her naked as quickly as possible.

Pulling her close, I slide my thumb up the inside of her thigh. Obediently, she parts her legs. It takes every measure of willpower I possess to keep from plunging straight into her wetness, but I want to draw it out. I want to tease her.

Instead, I draw small circles on her upper thigh, grazing her bare mound but not straying further. Soon her hips are rocking, and she moans in time with the movement of my hand.

Finally, I dip between her folds, groaning at the warm, slick welcome I find there.

Lifting my gaze, I enjoy her look of dazed pleasure and grin when she blinks open her pretty blue eyes to watch what I'm doing to her. "That's it, angel. Climb onto my lap and sing for me, huh?"

She moves back, straddling my legs and parting hers so her glorious pussy is spread open for me. She leans her head back on my shoulder and we both enjoy the view. Her high perky breasts rise and fall rapidly. Her lightly tanned skin is flushed a deeper shade across her chest and her cheeks.

Jessie's lips part when I stroke her. Using the light touches she likes best at first, I glide my thumb up and down her sex, teasing her entrance and skimming over her clit without pressing too firmly. When her hips roll to meet my finger, I increase the pressure and she reaches back, grasping my horn with her right hand. "Oh God, just like that. Just like that."

I kiss and nip at her neck as I speed my caresses. When I know she needs more, I give in, sliding one thick finger into her tight channel, then curl and massage the spongy inner walls.

Jessie cries out. Her pussy tenses around me. She closes her eyes.

"Watch, princess. I want you to watch how beautiful you are."

Wordlessly, she nods, opening her eyes to fix her gaze on the mirror. She tugs her lower lip between her teeth and my cock pulses against her ass. Lord, I need to be inside her. But not yet. Not yet. First she comes.

I maintain the steady motion and firm pressure, adding a second finger, until she is almost wild in my lap. After three more quick circles of my thumb around her clit, she moans my name, clenching and bucking. Her chest heaves. She grips me tight. My princess is coming for me over and over, letting out a long drawn out moan until, finally, she slumps back against my chest.

I give her a moment, then slowly I withdraw my fingers. Kissing her temple, I help her turn.

When she's got her arms around my neck and is looking down at me with a soft, fuck-drunk expression on her face, I look at her in wonder. This is it. It doesn't get any better than this.

Well, not until she grasps my aching cock and sinks down over me and I remember just how close to heaven it feels to be inside her. She squeezes me tight, brushing her lips over mine in a tender kiss. Then she rides my cock until I'm about ready to beg for mercy.

Sweet mercy, this woman is something else. If I could think beyond the mesmerizing motion of her hips as she slicks her pussy up and down my shaft, I could form better words to tell her what a treasure she is. As it is, I growl and grip her ass, praising her tight little pussy, her devious body.

"Mmm, so good. God, I love this cock."

Christ, if I thought I was having trouble holding on before, that was nothing. Her filthy, sweet words milk pleasure from me until my cock is throbbing inside her and my balls draw tight, ready to release.

She grins at me, then leans back and grinds her clit against my body. "I'm so close, babe. So close. Come with me?"

Fuck. Me.

In one swift movement, I gather her in my arms, keeping her impaled on my cock. Then, I turn and pound her into the bed. Wet slapping sounds fill the room and she whimpers. Her nails dig into my shoulders. Then she grips me tight, her body shuddering as she comes, taking me with her. I empty myself into her. My hips buck forward and I groan. Intense, perfect. My pleasure pours from me into her and she's still fluttering around me when I finish.

Lifting my weight from her with my hands on either side of the bed, I gaze down at her. "I'm so lucky to have found you."

Her flushed smile is everything I've ever wanted.

"And I'm lucky to have found you." The way she looks up at me, I actually start to believe it.

I pull from her carefully and fetch her a cloth to clean up. Then, I tuck her against my chest and we curl together on the bed while I stroke her hair. "My treasure. My everything."

Jessie sighs and snuggles closer. "And you're mine. I can't wait to find out what happens next. Now we're free to make our own story."

About the Author

Ami Wright is a proud history nerd, foodie and tragic fan of trashy reality TV, smutty romance, good wine and too much cake. She loves heroes who burn, pine and (think they're going to) perish for wanting their women, and heroines of every description!

Ami lives in Australia with her partner (who disappointingly is not called Mr Wright) and their two small children. If she ever gets any spare time between writing smut, teaching and mothering, she reads, cooks, watches history documentaries and dreams of the days when international travel becomes a reality again!

You can find out more and connect with Ami at:

http://linktr.ee/AmiWright

GIVEN TO THE GARGOYLE

Alien Protector's Lady
Alien Protector's Sunshine

Printed in Great Britain
by Amazon